CUPHEAD

in A MOUNTAIN OF TROUBLE

by Ron Bates

With Illustrations by Studio MDHR

Little, Brown and Company

New York Boston

© 2020 StudioMDHR Entertainment Inc. All Rights Reserved. Cuphead™, StudioMDHR™, and the StudioMDHR™ logo are trademarks and/or registered trademarks of StudioMDHR Entertainment Inc. throughout the world.

Art & Story Direction by Studio MDHR.
Cover design by Ching N. Chan & Studio MDHR.

Little, Brown and Company
Hachette Book Group
1290 Avenue of the Americas, New York, NY 10104
Visit us at LBYR.com

First Edition: December 2020

Little, Brown and Company is a division of Hachette Book Group, Inc. The Little, Brown name and logo are trademarks of Hachette Book Group, Inc.

The publisher is not responsible for websites (or their content) that are not owned by the publisher.

Library of Congress Control Number 2020945458

ISBNs: 978-0-316-49589-9 (paper over board), 978-0-316-49588-2 (ebook)

Printed in the United States of America

LSC-H

Printing 1, 2020

To Loretta Scott Crew, who made sitting around a campfire a million times better. Thanks for the s'mores.

—Ron Bates

For Doutzen, Hans, and Hugo. May your lives be filled with wondrous stories.

—Tata and Mama

CHALK IT UP TO SUMMERTIME

When Cuphead opened his eyes, he saw a bear. How the bear got inside the cabin is anyone's guess, but that's not important right now. What matters is there it was, big as life, hovering bearishly above the hammock where, until a moment earlier, Cuphead had been blissfully asleep. It was a large bear, as bears in cabins tend to be, and do you know what Cuphead did? Well, he did what anyone would have done if they suddenly woke up and found themselves staring at a set of teeth the size of piano keys.

He yawned.

This wasn't unusual, of course; lots of people yawn when they wake up in the morning. It's a very pleasant way to start the day. As for the bear, he smiled, straightened his bow tie (oh, by the way, the bear was wearing a bow tie), and picked up a plump, juicy pineapple. After shaking the fruit beside his

3

right ear, then by his left, he popped off the top and neatly inserted a straw and tiny umbrella.

He handed the refreshment to Cuphead, who took a long, nourishing sip.

"Shall I get the door for you, sir?" asked the bear.

"Don't bother, I'll take the shortcut," said Cuphead, and he leaped out the window.

The only problem was that this particular window was on the third floor (it was a very large cabin), and he appeared to be in for a terrible fall. But as luck would have it, just below him, a distinguished-looking badger was pushing a newly purchased four-poster bed home to his burrow. So after an exhilarating plunge, Cuphead helped himself to the softest landing he'd known in a long while, trampolined off the mattress, and bounded onto his feet.

And since it was such a nice day out, he went for a walk, and everywhere he walked he saw something fun. There were horses tossing horseshoes, and horseshoes tossing horses, and ants having a picnic, and gum trees blowing bubbles of every size and flavor. He saw fiddler crabs fiddling, bread slices loafing, faucets running, boxes boxing, sneakers sneaking, bumblebees bumbling, and an army of bullfrogs playing a game they called *croak-ay* (which is exactly like croquet, but noisier).

Just ahead, Cuphead's brother, Mugman, was giving flying lessons to a group of chickens. One by one, he'd load them into a gigantic slingshot and launch them into the stratosphere, where they'd drop their eggs like bombardiers over a target site. Meanwhile, Ms. Chalice, who was an excellent archer, would shoot an arrow into the air, crack the shells in mid-plunge, and catch the yolks in a skillet for breakfast. As Cuphead strolled by, she slid them onto his plate, and he happily ate his morning meal while continuing down the path.

At last, he arrived at an elm tree that had a large button on the side. It said UP. Cuphead, who could never resist a good button, pressed it, and in no time at all two doors opened like an elevator. He stepped inside. A moment later, he emerged at the top of the tree; walked out onto one of the long, springy branches; and bounced. He bounced not once, not twice, but three times, then did a perfect swan dive into the lake (oh, by the way, there was a lake) and disappeared under the cool, clear water. When he surfaced, he was on a pair of water skis, being pulled by two very helpful beavers in a motorboat. After a quick trip around the pond, he skied effortlessly onto the shore, put on a pair of sunglasses, and collapsed into a cabana chair underneath a big, flashy neon sign that said:

CAMP HOOTENHOLLER
A GREAT PLACE TO SIT AROUND AND DO NUTHIN'
(NO LOITERING)

As Cuphead lay there, sipping pineapple juice and relaxing in the breeze, the most beautiful songbird he had ever seen opened her lovely mouth and—

"Cuphead! CUPHEAD!"

Oh dear, that didn't sound like a songbird at all. It sounded like the voice of his teacher, Professor Lucien, because that's exactly what it was. Suddenly, Camp Hootenholler and all its wonderful delights vanished, and Cuphead found himself sitting at his very ordinary desk surrounded by his equally ordinary classmates.

Professor Lucien stood at the blackboard. He looked irritated.

"Cuphead," he said sternly, "if you're not too busy daydreaming, perhaps you could come up here and show us the answer to our math problem."

Math problem? On the last day of school? Surely

he was joking. Cuphead couldn't possibly do math now. He'd already cleared his mind of anything remotely educational. Why, he'd spent all last evening emptying his brain of history, arithmetic, and the location of his gym locker. It wasn't something he wanted to do, you understand, but he had to make room for more important things—camp nicknames, for example. After all, you couldn't show up at a top-notch place like Camp Hootenholler without some catchy nicknames to throw around. So far he'd come up with Stilts, Curly, Pencilneck, Wisenheimer, Half-Pint, Moonbeam, Bookworm, and The Sarsaparilla Kid. He could hardly wait to find campers to pin them on. So obviously, at this particular moment, answering any question that wasn't in some way nickname-related would be a complete waste of time.

He was surprised Professor Lucien, one of the smartest people on the Inkwell Isles, hadn't realized that himself. Then again, nobody's perfect.

"Did you hear me, Cuphead?" the professor asked.

"Um, sure, I heard ya," said Cuphead. "I was just, uh, tying my shoelaces."

Professor Lucien rubbed the temples of his bulb.

"You don't have shoelaces, Cuphead."

This was an excellent point. Cuphead examined his feet.

"Oh," he said at last. "That's probably why it's taking so long."

And having no other choice, he climbed out of his chair and started a slow, torturous walk toward the front of the class. On the way, he tried very hard not to think about Camp Hootenholler, because that would only make doing math a thousand times harder, but—

"*Psssst*, Cuphead," said Ms. Chalice. "What's the secret Hootenholler handshake?"

Cuphead sighed. Ms. Chalice was his very best friend in the world, but she had an annoying habit of getting him into trouble. Take now, for instance. She knew perfectly well the secret Hootenholler handshake was two shakes, a moose call, and a smack on the head with a rubber mallet. For cryin' out loud, they'd practiced it a dozen times! But like everyone else in their class, she was bursting with excitement about going to camp, and wanted to make sure nothing would go wrong. Of course, Cuphead would've gladly helped her, but she couldn't have picked a worse time. Professor Lucien was waiting! So when Ms. Chalice extended her hand, Cuphead ignored it, put the whole thing out of his mind, and tried to remember what a plus sign looked like.

The next thing he knew, he was standing at the blackboard.

"All right, Cuphead," said Professor Lucien. "If *A* equals three, and *B* equals nine, and *C* equals twenty-seven, what does *D* equal?"

Well, that was strange. Cuphead could see his teacher's lips moving, but the words coming out were complete gobbledygook. A *equals three?* B *equals nine?* What was he talking about? And why was he mixing together letters and numbers, which everyone knows are two entirely different things? Cuphead felt sorry for the poor professor. Perhaps he needed a vacation, maybe to some kind of wonderful camp where they had butler bears, and elm-levators, and bullfrogs playing—

No, no, no, no, no! Cuphead couldn't think about that right now. He had to concentrate on the math problem! So he gritted his teeth and squinted his eyes until he'd squeezed even the name of ol' Camp Whatchamacallit right out of his brain. And when he was ready, he picked up the chalk and wrote a large letter *D* on the blackboard, then glanced hopefully at the professor. Professor Lucien crossed his arms and tapped his foot. So next to the *D*, Cuphead drew two parallel lines, which he vaguely remembered being the way you make an equal sign. He was very pleased with how it turned out. It's funny, though. He'd never noticed before how much the equal sign looks like a pair of water skis. The resemblance was uncanny. And speaking of water skis, he happened to know of a place where they had the most incredible waterskiing you'll ever see, a little slice of paradise called Camp Hooten—

NO, NO, NO! It was not a pair of water skis; it was an equal sign. A plain, ordinary, dull-as-dry-cereal equal sign, and it had absolutely nothing to do with motorboats or beavers or that camp whose name he definitely couldn't recall right now. Cuphead was done with that nonsense, and he quickly returned to the business of staring very hard at the equation on the board and hoping for a miracle. And to his great surprise, he was just about to come up with the answer when, *"Psssssssst!"*

He heard a noise.

"Psssssssssssssssst!"

Against his better judgment, Cuphead turned around. When he did, he saw that his classmates had formed themselves into a pyramid in the middle of the room, and Mugman was leading them in a cheer.

Marshmallows, wiener roasts, sis–boom–bah!
Hootenholler! Hootenholler! Rah, rah, RAH!

Cuphead groaned. This was agony.

"The equation," Professor Lucien reminded him.

Ah, yes, the equation. He could stall no longer. After a deep breath, he raised the chalk; made a big, bold, somewhat-numeric-looking line; and—

RINGGGGGGGGG!

Yes! Saved by the bell! That glorious, magnificent, ear-splitting bell! Summer had arrived and the terrible, unsolvable math problem no longer had any power over him. Quickly, he grabbed the *D* he had drawn on the chalkboard and turned it sideways so it looked like a little boat.

"Come on!" he yelled, and an instant later, he, Ms. Chalice, and Mugman were all sitting in the *D*-shaped tub.

"Just a moment," said Professor Lucien, giving them a serious look. Then he picked up the chalk and drew a life preserver.

"Safety first," he said.

Cuphead took it and grinned. And with that, the three friends waved goodbye to the professor, sailed across the blackboard, and floated out the schoolhouse door.

2

READY FOR ANYTHING

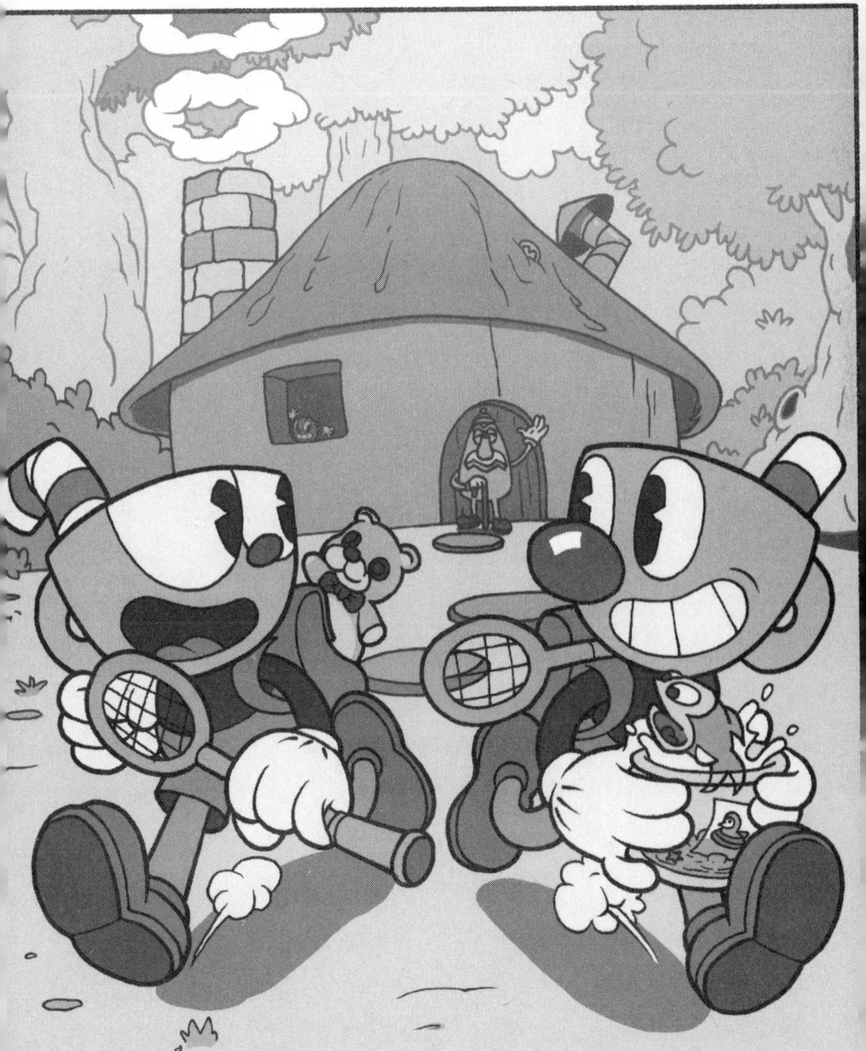

When the boys arrived back home, Cuphead went straight up to his room, and Mugman went, well... straight up.

"WHOAAAAAAAAAA!"

Hearing the sudden cry, Elder Kettle (who was the boys' guardian and knew shenanigans when he heard them) rushed to investigate. What he found was Mugman hanging upside down from the parlor ceiling with his foot caught in the grip of an elaborate trap.

"CUP-HEAD!" Elder Kettle bellowed.

Naturally, Cuphead came racing down the stairs. Elder Kettle gave him a long, disapproving glare.

"Cuphead, what is the meaning of this?"

Cuphead gulped.

It wasn't what Elder Kettle said exactly. It was the way he said it. He had that tone, the one that sounded like a pirate making you walk the plank because you forgot to bring the scary-looking flag with the skeleton on it. It was an awful sound, and Cuphead felt sick to his stomach. He hadn't meant to do anything wrong; he'd just been excited about going to camp and wanted to practice capturing wild beasts.

He stared at the floor.

"I'm sorry," he said.

Elder Kettle sighed and shook his head.

"Well, I should think you would be," he grumbled. "You call that a snare?"

"What?" asked Cuphead.

"A snare, boy. A snare!" said the kettle. "This will never do. See how flimsy that rope is? Oh, it's fine for catching your brother, but what if Mugman had been a hippopotamus, or a whale?"

"Or a vending machine," said Mugman, who had begun to twirl around in a little circle.

"Or a vending machine," Elder Kettle agreed. "This is the wilderness, boy! You need to be ready for anything. I remember my days at Hootenholler. Why, I caught things twice the size of Mugman! Here, let me show you how it's done."

And for the next hour and a quarter, Cuphead and Elder Kettle stood there making snares and

16

catching Mugman and all the other ferocious things they happened to find in the cottage. They caught a dining room set, two wing chairs, a sewing machine, the coat rack, and that nice young fellow who was selling vacuum cleaners door to door.

When they'd finished, Elder Kettle poured himself a cup of tea and sat down at the recently liberated kitchen table.

"Camp Hootenholler!" he said proudly. "You boys are in for one terrific summer. Gosh, I wish I were going with you!"

Elder Kettle went on and on about Camp Hootenholler, pouring out fond memories of his days there. Of course, that was some time ago, but he was sure it would be just as thrilling now.

"Oh, the fun we had," he recalled. "Me, Sawbuck, Dumpy, Scooter—the whole gang."

Sawbuck? Dumpy? Those were camp nicknames! Cuphead suddenly became very excited.

"Did you have a camp nickname, Elder Kettle?" he asked.

Elder Kettle stroked his chin.

"Well, let me see. It has been a while, you know," he said. "Ah, yes—Yo-Yo. They all called me Yo-Yo."

Yo-Yo. It was an excellent nickname! Cuphead made a mental note.

"Why did they call you Yo-Yo?" asked Mugman. "Can you do amazing tricks?"

"Can I do amazing tricks?" roared Elder Kettle, and he promptly pulled a yo-yo from his pocket, flung it to the floor, and realized, no, he couldn't do amazing tricks. "Oh well, it doesn't matter because that's not why they called me Yo-Yo. They called me Yo-Yo because of my yodeling. I was the best yodeler in the whole camp!"

Cuphead and Mugman were very impressed, and they would've been even more so if they'd had the slightest idea what a yodeler was. But they didn't.

Elder Kettle stared at their blank, confused faces.

"Come now, surely you know what yodeling is?"

They shook their heads.

"You mean you've never heard a yodel? Then are you in for a treat!" he told them. "Why, it's candy for your eardrums—it's the music of the mountains!"

And just like that, Elder Kettle climbed on top of the kitchen table, puffed out his chest, and—

"*YOOOO-dle-Yug-doo-LAHHHHH-hee-urgggggggggg-a-LArt!*"

Cuphead couldn't believe what he was hearing. It sounded like someone was badly mistreating a goose. If Elder Kettle was the best yodeler at Camp Hootenholler, he would hate to meet the second best.

The old kettle climbed off the table and looked at the boys. They were speechless. Then wordless. Then phraseless. Then soundless. Finally, when they'd completely run out of noises not to make, Mugman burst into applause and yelled, "Hooray!"

He didn't say "hooray" because he liked Elder Kettle's performance; he said it because he liked Elder Kettle. Mugman wouldn't hurt Elder Kettle for anything.

As for Cuphead, he cheered, as well. It was only polite. Besides, he'd never heard anyone yodel before—maybe it was supposed to sound like that? He tried to think of something nice to say, but nothing came to mind. Then Elder Kettle turned to him with his warm eyes and cheery grin, and all of a sudden Cuphead knew.

"You're one in a million, Yo-Yo," he said.

And that much, at least, was true.

The kettle smiled and took a humble bow.

"Well, I guess you boys better start getting your gear together," he said. "It's almost time."

He was right. The bus would be here any minute. Cuphead could hardly believe it was happening. They were going to Camp Hootenholler! He started up the stairs and was halfway to the top when he realized Mugman wasn't following. His brother was just standing there in the parlor gazing up at Elder Kettle.

"It is a nice camp, isn't it?" he said at last.

Elder Kettle wrinkled up his brow. Hadn't the boy been listening? How could he even ask such a thing? But then he remembered that Mugman was very young, and this would be his first time away from home, and that wasn't easy even for the bravest of mugs. And that's when his grand old face softened, and he smiled and put a reassuring hand on Mugman's shoulder.

"Nice? Why, it's a showplace. It's the finest camp in the whole wide world. They have the friendliest staff, the comfiest cabins, and the most delicious food you've ever tasted. You've got absolutely nothing to worry about, my boy."

Mugman looked very relieved.

"Except, of course, for the bad things," said Elder Kettle.

Mugman gulped. Meanwhile, his brother backed slowly down the stairs.

"Bad things?" Cuphead said.

"Did I say bad things?" asked the old kettle. "I meant terrible things. Despicable things. Pesky bugs, tumbling boulders, poisonous plants, and, of course, the Punchafinks. Oh, believe me, the last thing you want to do is run into a Punchafink."

Cuphead ambled across the room until he stood directly in front of his guardian.

"Um," he said, "what's a Punchafink?"

Elder Kettle gasped.

"What's a Punchafink? Why, it's the most awful thing you'll ever meet! It's a real menace, that's what it is. Take it from me, the Punchafinks are your worst nightmare."

But before Elder Kettle could explain, a clanking, clunking, sputtering, puttering noise erupted outside the cottage. When Cuphead opened the front door, he saw a rickety old bus, and hanging from one of its windows was Ms. Chalice.

"Well, what are you waitin' for?" she shouted. "Let's get shakin'!"

In a flash, Cuphead and Mugman streaked up the stairs. When they came down again, they were carrying large packs overstuffed with fishing rods, tennis rackets, comic books, a camera, hiking boots, sunglasses, sleeping bags, a goldfish bowl, and two changes of underwear. They yelled a quick goodbye to Elder Kettle as they raced out the door.

"Goodbye, boys! Have a wonderful time," Elder Kettle called from the doorway. "And oh, I almost forgot—beware the curse of the mountain!"

"Curse?" said Mugman, stopping in his tracks.

The bus started to pull away.

"Mugman?" Cuphead said.

But his brother did not move. The bus rolled faster.

"Mugman?" Cuphead said again.

"Mugman!"

And this time, he grabbed his sibling by the collar and dragged him quickly down the street and through the open door of the moving bus.

"Whew! Made it," cried Cuphead, and for the first time in a long time, it seemed all their troubles were behind them.

But of course, on the Inkwell Isles, things are seldom as they seem.

3

A BUMP IN THE ROAD

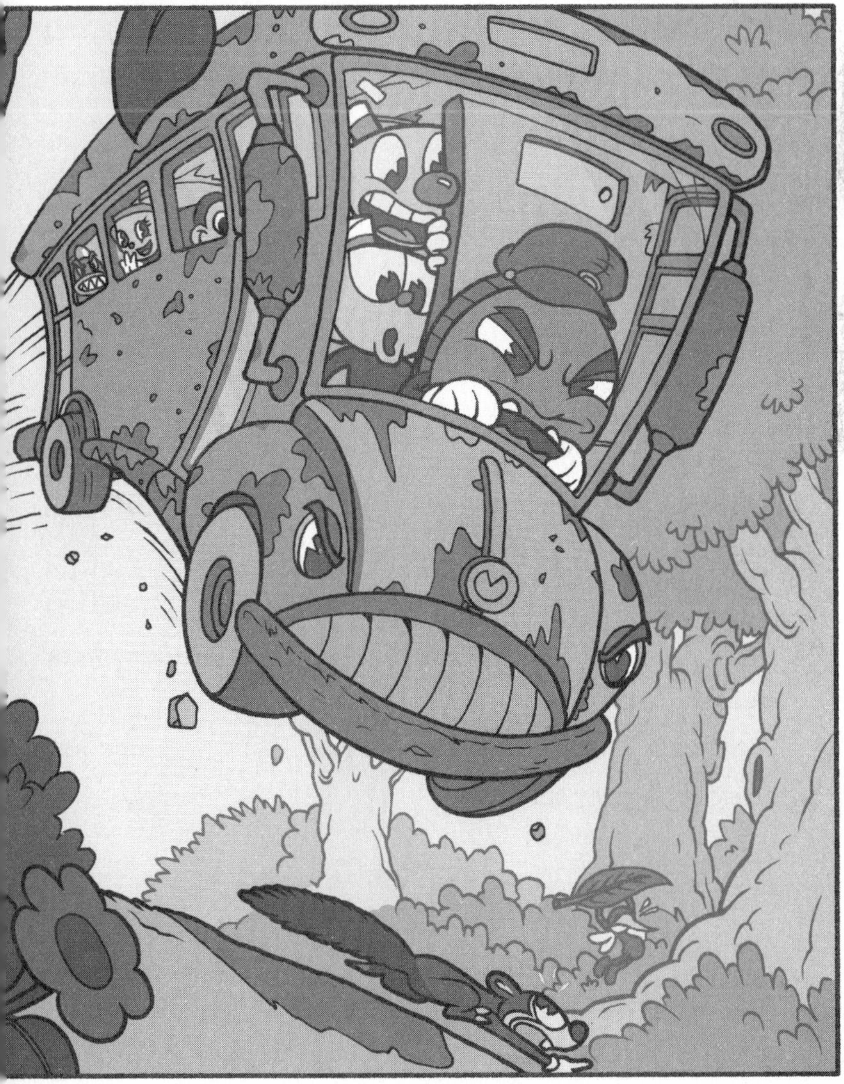

N umber four," said the bus driver.

Cuphead knew it was the bus driver because he was sitting behind the wheel and he wore a little cap. Also, he was completely round and very shiny, but that didn't matter since bus drivers come in all shapes and sizes.

"I beg your pardon?" said Cuphead.

"Number four!" the driver said again, and he pointed to a sheet of paper posted on the divider beside his seat.

Cuphead looked at the page. It was yellow and had big black letters at the top. It said: EXTREMELY IMPORTANT AND SERIOUS RULES FOR BUS PASSENGERS! YOU WILL NOTICE THAT WE HAVE USED EXCLAMATION POINTS AND VERY FANCY PAPER. THAT'S HOW IMPORTANT THESE RULES ARE!

Well, as anyone will tell you, yellow papers with

exclamation points are nothing to sneeze at. Cuphead glanced at the bus driver.

"Do you mean you want me to read rule number four?" Cuphead asked.

The driver rolled his eyes and held up four fingers, which was no help at all.

So Cuphead shrugged and turned his attention back to the yellow page. It had a list of rules numbered one to thirty-seven and many, many punctuation marks and no pictures. And since any list of thirty-seven well-punctuated anythings without a single picture was bound to be extremely official, he thought he'd better start at the very beginning.

The first line read, RULE NUMBER 1: NO STOWAWAYS! IF YOU ARE A STOWAWAY, THEN SHAME ON YOU, AND WE WILL BE VERY RUDE WHEN WE ASK YOU TO LEAVE. ALSO, YOU DO NOT GET TO READ THE REST OF THE RULES.

Tough but fair, thought Cuphead, and he looked at the next one.

RULE NUMBER 2: NO SINGING SILLY BUS-RIDING SONGS.

"Now, by silly bus-riding songs, do you mean—"

he began, but the bus driver stopped him and pointed to rule number three.

NO ASKING THE BUS DRIVER GOOFY QUESTIONS.

Cuphead wanted to ask the driver how he knew his question was going to be goofy but then wondered if that might be an even goofier question. After all, he didn't want to get a reputation as a rule breaker before they even got to camp. So he ignored the interruption and moved on to rule number four.

WE HAVE GONE TO GREAT EXPENSE TO EQUIP THIS VEHICLE WITH SPECIALIZED SITTING DEVICES CALLED "SEATS." AND IF YOU DO NOT USE THEM, THE DRIVER WILL BE VERY GRUMPY.

"Did you read rule number four?" asked the bus driver, who seemed fairly grumpy already.

"Yes," said Cuphead.

"Good," said the driver. "THEN SIT DOWN!"

Suddenly, the bus hit a bump in the road, and the boys were propelled through the air, down the aisle, and into a specialized sitting device. When they turned around, they saw Ms. Chalice.

"Well, look who decided to drop in," she said. "I see you met Ol' Smiley."

She meant the bus driver, of course. It was an odd thing to call him, not just because his name was Quint—which it was—but because he hadn't smiled once since they'd gotten on the bus. Ms. Chalice, you see, was being sarcastic. That's when someone says the opposite of what they really mean, like calling a shrimp "Jumbo" or a bald eagle "Harry." This happens a lot more often than you'd think and almost always hurts their feelings.

"Eh, he's just a sourpuss," said Cuphead. "Don't worry about him. When we get to the camp, everything's going to be aces, right, Mugman? Mugman?"

But Mugman wasn't listening. He was just staring out into space, dreamlike, pondering a single question over and over in his brain.

"Cuphead, what did Elder Kettle mean by 'the curse of the mountain'? What did he mean, Cuphead?" he said.

Oh yes, the curse. With all the excitement of getting on the bus, Cuphead had completely forgotten about it.

"Who knows? It's probably just some dumb ol' legend," he told his brother. "Camps are full of stories like that—it's part of the fun. You wait and see. I bet they'll try to spook us with some malarkey about that old curse when we get there. And when they do, you

28

can take it right over to the mess hall and put it on a sandwich, because it's a hundred percent baloney!"

Being the older brother, Cuphead knew all about these things, and Mugman felt much better. As for Ms. Chalice—

"Mess hall?" she asked.

"It's where they serve the grub. You know, the dining room."

"Mess hall," she repeated with a slightly squeamish look on her face. "Sounds charming."

About that time, the bus hit another bump in the road, and everyone bounced up in their seats like popcorn kernels on a hot skillet.

"Speaking of messes," Ms. Chalice said, "this bus doesn't sound so good."

"Or look so good," said Mugman.

"Or smell so good," said everyone with a nose.

Cuphead had been thinking the same thing. He didn't know why, but he'd expected the bus to be as amazing as everything else at Camp Hootenholler. But this one had lumpy tires and wobbly bumpers and rusty springs, and it smelled like a burning baseball glove. Also, some of the letters had fallen off the side so it looked like they were going to CAMP OOT N

OLLER, which was embarrassing. Unless, of course, they'd gotten on the wrong bus and really were going to CAMP OOT N OLLER.

The engine made a belching noise, and the whole bus filled up with black smoke.

Oh, please let there be a CAMP OOT N OLLER, Cuphead thought.

When the smoke cleared, the three friends rushed to the window and gasped for air. As they gazed down the road behind them, they saw their little town fading into the distance. Now they were in the countryside, and instead of houses and buildings, they saw flowers and meadows and trees. It was an awfully nice day, and just looking at the natural beauty of the Inkwell Isles made them excited for camp all over again.

"You know, this ol' bus ain't so bad," Ms. Chalice said. "All we need is some entertainment. Hey, everybody, how 'bout a game of looky looky?"

In one great burst, the bus riders all leaped to their feet and stomped and clapped and cheered! Nothing passed the time quite like staring out the window and giving clues about something you saw there. But just as Ms. Chalice opened her mouth to say *Looky looky, I see something round as a cookie*, she was cut off by a particularly loud throat clearing.

"No dice, girlie!" said Quint, who appeared to be smiling for the first time in his life. "Rule nineteen!"

Cuphead squinted at the yellow paper. Sure enough, there it was.

RULE NUMBER 19: NO PLAYING GAMES, ESPECIALLY ONES THAT MAKE YOU LOOK AT THINGS. EYESTRAIN IS NOT OUR IDEA OF FUN!

The passengers let out a collective groan. They were beginning to think that sitting on a bus for a very long period of time was not as exciting as it sounded. Surely there was something they could do. As the miles passed, they tried face painting, finger puppets, knitting, glass blowing, clog dancing, gourmet cookery, candlepin bowling, and reenacting the great naval battles of history. But each time, Quint would raise his hand, scowl, and point sternly to the yellow paper.

"That bus driver is becoming a real pain in the specialized sitting device," said Cuphead.

Mugman nodded, because he was in complete agreement. But Ms. Chalice? She just grinned.

"Leave it to me," she said.

And with a wink, she ducked down in her seat. When she popped up again, she was in the back of the bus wearing a waist-length jacket and a little flat-top cap.

"Telegram!" she called.

And then she was gone again. A second later, she popped up in another row.

"Telegram!"

And another.

"Telegram!"

In short order, she popped out of six suitcases, three lunch boxes, and the glove compartment. Quint's eyes darted from place to place to place as they chased after her, but she was always a little too quick. Then, just when he'd lost track of her entirely, he heard a loud *THUD!*

Ms. Chalice was on the windshield. *Telegram!* she mouthed.

The next thing Quint knew, she was sitting on his steering wheel.

"Telegram for Mr. Quint," she called.

"Mr. Quint? Hey, that's me!" he said.

You couldn't blame him for being excited. People as unfriendly as Quint rarely get mail of any kind, much less a telegram. He eagerly signed the receipt book, and Ms. Chalice, in the most professional way possible, held out a neatly sealed envelope.

"Oh boy, oh boy, oh boy, oh boy, oh boy!" Quint squealed, and reached for his telegram.

And that's when Ms. Chalice jerked it away.

"*Ohhhhhhhhh*, will you look at that?" she said. "What a shame. I really wish I could give this to you, but darn—it's against the rules!"

And she stuffed the envelope back inside her pocket.

"Wait!" begged Quint. "There must be some mistake."

But Ms. Chalice shook her head and pointed to the fancy yellow paper with the thirty-eight very important and serious rules. What's that? You thought there were only thirty-seven very important and serious rules? Well, you are to be congratulated because you're absolutely right. There *were* only thirty-seven, but when Quint looked at the list, he saw that something new had been added to the bottom in bright-red crayon.

RULE NUMBER 38: NO TELEGRAMS!!! it said.

Quint's face turned the color of an overripe

tomato. He mumbled. Then he grumbled. Then he bristled, and boiled, and blubbered.

"Rules, schmoolz!" he said at last, and ripped the yellow paper into a million pieces. "Now gimme, gimme, gimme, gimme, gimme, gimme, gimme!"

Ms. Chalice smiled and handed him the envelope. Quint couldn't wait to open it up, and when he did—

"Hello!"
"Helloooo!"
"Helloooooo!"
"Helloooooooooo!"

Out popped the Four Mel Arrangement. You see, the four Mels—Mel, Melvin, Melroy, and Melbert— were a very famous barbershop quartet. You've probably heard of them (and if you haven't, you obviously need to spend more time in musical barbershops). And since this was a singing telegram, the Mels wasted no time at all in belting out a silly bus-riding song.

QUINT*'s the greatest* BUS *driver*
Bus driver, bus driver
QUINT*'s the greatest* BUS *driver*

We've ever seen—
He's GROUCHY, *he's* GRUMPY
The RIDE *is so* BUMPY—
But QUIIIIIIIINT's *the greatest* BUS *driver*
We've ever seen!
He RIPPED *up the* PAPER
The RULES *turned to* VAPOR—
So QUIIIIIIIINT's *the greatest* BUS *driver*
We've ever seen!
He's KIND *of a* YELLER
But STILL *a* FINE FELLER—
Oh, QUIIIIIIIINT's *the greatest* BUS *driver*
We've ever seen!
He GAVE *us an* EARFUL
Just CUZ *we were* CHEERFUL—
Oh, QUIIIIIIIINT's *the greatest* BUS *driver*
We've ever seen!

Everyone sang along at the top of their lungs, while Quint scowled in the grouchiest way you can imagine and said the most terrible things under his breath. But what could he do? There was no rule against singing silly bus-riding songs. In fact, there were no rules at all.

The RULES *were so* BORING
But NOW *we are* ROARING—
Oh, QUIIIIIIIINT*'s the greatest* BUS *driver*
We've ever seen!
WE'VE *almost* FORGOTTEN
That HE *acted* ROTTEN—
Oh, QUIIIIIIIINT*'s the greatest* BUS *driver*
We've ever seen!

As the campers traveled down the road, their singing grew louder and louder, and before long, the flowers and trees and billboards and stop signs were all dancing and swaying to the happy sound. Why, even the clanky old bus couldn't resist.

"Vroom! Vroom! Cha-cha-cha. Vroom! Vroom! Cha-cha-cha," she hummed as she shimmied through the countryside.

And she kept right on shimmying until she came to a sudden and inconvenient stop.

Quint grunted and glared at the passengers.

"Now you've done it," he said. "You and your singing. How are we supposed to get up Nosebleed Hill?"

It was a timely question because Nosebleed Hill was right in front of them. Cuphead stared at it in awe.

It was by far the steepest, straightest, most stomach-churning hill on the Inkwell Isles. He was fairly sure the old bus would've had trouble going up it anytime, much less when she was all tuckered out from dancing.

Quint blew the horn.

"Come on, let's get movin'!" he yelled.

"Uh-uh...uh-uh...uh-uh," chugged the bus, and she would not budge an inch.

Cuphead scrunched up his nose. He wasn't one to give up when the going got tough, and nothing—not even Nosebleed Hill—was going to keep him from Camp Hootenholler.

"This ol' bus just needs a little encouragement!" he said. "Come on, everybody! Let's give her a hand!"

And believe it or not, every one of them—the campers, the Mels, and even Quint—joined together in a rousing chant.

"You can do it! You can do it! You can do it!"

It was a real battle cry, the kind that would inspire courage in the most timid of vehicles. And like magic, the old bus felt a new sense of confidence. Bumper-to-bumper confidence! She squinted her headlights and gritted her grill and—with a clang and a clunk and a boom—began to roll forward.

The chanters became very excited.

"You're going to make it! You're going to make it! You're going to make it!" they sang.

Their words filled the tank like musical fuel. The engine roared, the tires smoked, and sweat poured down her windshield, but the mighty bus kept climbing!

"You're almost there! You're almost there! You're almost there!"

With every passing second, the group drew closer to their destination. Cuphead stuck his head out the window and found he could actually see the top of the hill! A cheer went up from the passengers, and then—

"Oh boy...oh boy...oh boy!" chugged the bus.

They rolled backward.

This wasn't an ordinary roll, you understand. It was a full-fledged, high-speed, downhill plunge. The bus was moving faster and faster, but the plucky campers kept right on chanting.

"We're going to crash! We're going to crash! We're going to crash!"

And just when it seemed things couldn't get worse— they did. With a screech and a skitter and a skid, the bus spun completely off the road and over the edge of a cliff. The riders shrieked as they plummeted down, down, down until finally—

PLOP!

They landed. Well, maybe *landed* isn't the right word. It was more like they'd planted themselves in the ground, which is why the bus was standing straight up like a candle on a birthday cake.

"I think we fell into a hole," said Cuphead.

It was a logical conclusion since they were clearly stuck in something, and when it came to getting things stuck in them, nothing was better than holes.

But Canteen Hughes, who was a classmate and very good at geology, shook his head.

"It's not a hole," he said, adjusting his thick goggles and tightening his cap. "It's a geyser."

He was right, of course. It was a geyser, but not just any geyser—it was Old Forceful, the WORLD'S SPEWIEST GEYSER, or at least that's what it said on the billboards they'd passed along the road. And here they were stuck in its spout. Oh, what a terrible predicament! Not only were they unable to continue their journey (Quint was furiously revving the engine, but the bus wasn't going anywhere), they were very much in danger.

You see, despite their favorable reputation with tourists, geysers are not at all friendly. They are, in fact, real hotheads with the most abominable tempers. You've probably heard stories about how they fume and

39

fuss and then, at the slightest provocation, send torrents of steam and scalding water spewing into the air.

"We'll be roasted!" said Mugman, a declaration that caused a small riot inside the extremely vertical vehicle.

The campers rushed to the front of the bus and surrounded Quint.

"This is all your fault!" snapped Ginger, a normally sweet gingerbread girl who suddenly felt an urgent need to blame someone. "Why did you have to tear up those rules? Oh, our precious, precious rules!"

They all agreed that, in hindsight, the rules were very just and fair, and that Quint—in a moment of shocking irresponsibility—had doomed them all.

"Me?" Quint roared. "Hey, I wasn't the one who—"

He did not finish his thought. It seemed pointless now since, even at his loudest and angriest, he could never compete with the sound happening just outside the bus.

It was a rumble—a low, deep, terrifying rumble. Cuphead carefully opened the window.

"Excuse me, um, Old Forceful," he said. "We seem to be stuck in your face."

The geyser said nothing, but the ground shook and the rumble grew. Cuphead gripped the edge of the window.

"Anyhoo," he continued, "since you're probably busy and we've got places to be, I wondered if you might give us—"

"GIVE YOU WHAT?" boomed the geyser.

Cuphead gulped.

"A push," he said.

For a moment, nothing happened. Then the ground shook again, and the shaking got bigger, and then all the campers heard the unmistakable sound of laughter.

"HA! HA! HA! HA! HA!" Old Forceful chortled. "SO YOU WANT A PUSH, EH? SURE, I'LL GIVE YOU A PUSH!"

And without so much as a warning, the old blowhard sent huge billows of steam bursting up from the ground. Next, there was a thunderous sound, and the temperature rose so quickly that the bus, like a thermometer sticking out of a feverish mouth, turned bright red. After what seemed like forever, the campers heard a gurgle, then a pop, and, finally, a very, very, very loud *VOOOOOOOOOSH!*

Old Forceful erupted! In an instant, they were soaring across the sky like a big, boxy missile. Quint repeatedly blew the horn, surprising several birds who had not expected to find a clanky old camp bus flying through

41

their neighborhood. The rickety rocket climbed and climbed, and just when it seemed like they'd be spending the summer building campfires on the moon, it tipped forward and made a steep, harrowing dive. Quint stepped on the brake pedal, the passengers screamed, and a nervous suitcase bailed out using a spare undershirt as a parachute, but in the end, the old tub touched down with a bump and a bounce at the very top of Nosebleed Hill.

Naturally, being good campers, the group picked up their song right where they'd left off.

> *He* CRASHED *in a* GEYSER, *but* CAME OUT *the* WISER—
> *Oh,* QUIIIIIINT's *the* GREAT-*est* BUS *driver* WE'VE *ever* SEEN!

Quint pouted. He didn't care for this song at all. But it didn't matter because the campers went right on singing, and the bus went right on swaying, and they all went right on having a wonderful time until they reached a big wooden arch with a shiny brass sign. Cuphead pressed his face against the glass as he read the words:

WELCOME TO CAMP HOOTENHOLLER.

4

A BAD FIRST IMPRESSION

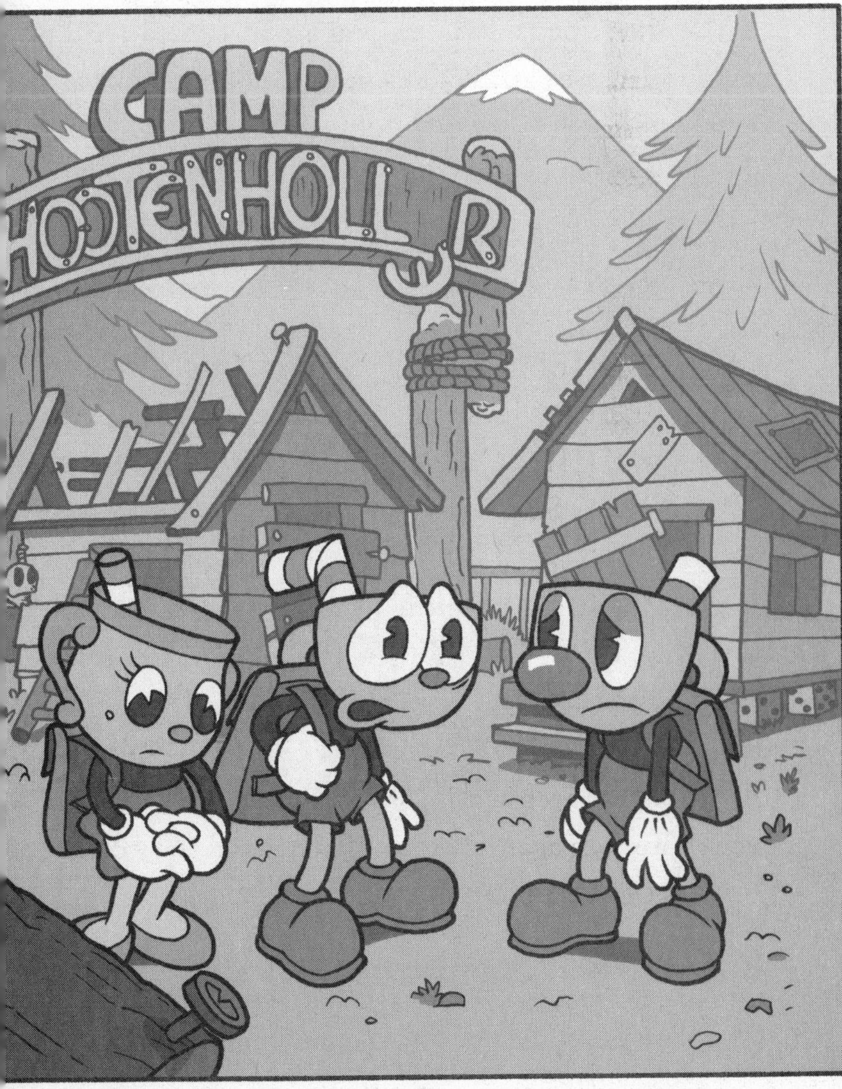
CAMP
HOOTENHOLL R

W e're here!" shouted the campers, and they all
stood up in their seats and did the traditional
camp-entering dance, which happened to be the
jitterbug.

Of course, no one was more excited than Cuphead.
He streaked across the ceiling, blazed a trail down the
aisle, and broke through the rear of the bus. When the
other campers peeked out through the large Cuphead-
shaped hole, they saw him on his hands and knees
kissing the ground.

"Ah, Hootenholler!" he said, smacking the earth.
"Mmm-WAH! Mmm-WAH! Mmm-WAH!"

It was the sweetest soil he had ever tasted, and when
he was done, he climbed to his feet and smiled. Then
he spit out an earthworm.

"Hey, what's the big idea?" yelled the worm, who

frowned ferociously and gave a very rude "Hmph!" before vanishing down his hole.

Oh dear, thought Cuphead. This was certainly not the way he'd wanted to begin his summertime adventure (and the worm was even less happy about it), but it didn't matter. He'd arrived at the place of his dreams, and all was right with the world. At last, he could turn and get his very first look at the storied Camp Hootenholler!

He took a deep breath.

"It's...it's...it's—"

"It's a wreck," said Mugman.

And sadly, he was right.

Poor Cuphead. He just stood there staring out at the disappointing landscape. It was nothing like the camp in his daydreams. There were no neon signs or high-rise cabins or very proper bears serving pineapples on silver platters. Instead, there were boarded-up windows and weeds the size of cornstalks and bits of litter that had somehow managed to reach every location except the inside of a garbage can.

"Wowsers, it's a ghost town," said Ms. Chalice, because it looked like a ghost town, and also because there was a ghost in it.

He was just sitting there on a bench reading the morning edition of the *Inkwell Daily Boos* (which is the only newspaper ghosts really enjoy). So, not wanting to seem unfriendly, Ms. Chalice went over to say hello.

"Good afternoon," she said. "We just—"

"Evening," interrupted the ghost.

"Excuse me?"

"It isn't afternoon, it's evening," he told her, and he went back to reading his paper.

Ms. Chalice frowned. She had forgotten how irritating ghosts could be—always creaking boards or rattling chains or correcting your grammar. It was very annoying. Of course, Ms. Chalice knew all about ghosts, having once been part of the spirit world herself, but that's another story.

"Oh, right. Good *eeeeevening*," she said, deliberately emphasizing the word. "Anyway, we just got off the bus, and we were wondering about the camp. Do you live here?"

"I'm a ghost. I don't *live* anywhere," said the ghost.

Ms. Chalice bit her bottom lip.

"I didn't mean *live* live," she said. "I just thought you might know where we're supposed to put our things. We're the new campers."

"Campers?!"

The ghost turned as white as a sheet. Or maybe he didn't—it's hard to tell with ghosts.

"No, no, no, that's impossible!" he said. "This camp is occupied, and we are not sharing it with anyone."

Ms. Chalice was confused.

"We?"

"Of course, *we*," he told her. "I'm here with my troop. We're ghost scouts."

Now, if you've never heard of the Ghost Scouts (and most people haven't), it's an organization that encourages ghosts to spend more time outdoors for some reason. Ms. Chalice never really understood why since ghosts hate sunshine and have absolutely no use for fresh air, but if it got them out of the city for a while, it was perfectly all right with her.

What wasn't all right was having them take over her camp.

"This isn't fair!" she complained. "Me and my friends have come a long, long way!"

"Tough tombstones," said the ghost. "We were here first. Also, we have a reservation. Also, it's not 'me and my friends,' it's 'my friends and I,' which has nothing to do with the camping situation, but it was bothering me."

Uh-oh. Now he'd done it. Ms. Chalice's eyes narrowed until they were as thin as coin slots, and her face turned jalapeño red. If some know-it-all ghost thought he could tell her how to speak, and what to say, and where she would be spending her summer, he was very much mistaken.

She gave the ghoulish gasbag her most menacing glare.

"Listen, wisenheimer," she said through clenched teeth. "ME AND MY FRIENDS are tired! ME AND MY FRIENDS are hungry! ME AND MY FRIENDS have been looking forward to this all year, and ME AND MY FRIENDS are going to stay right here at Camp Hootenholler!"

Oh goodness. Such an outburst was very unlike Ms. Chalice, who prided herself on never being rude to people she'd just met, not even extremely irritating ghosts. But when she glanced at the spectral figure, she noticed he did not appear to be offended by her words—in fact, he seemed unusually pleased.

"Did you say 'Hootenholler'?" he asked.

Ms. Chalice cocked an eyebrow.

"So what if I did?"

"You mean this isn't Camp Haunt 'n' Howler?"

"Haunt 'n' Howler?" she said. "Of course not."

"Oh, thank ghoulness!" said the ghost, and he leaped up from the bench and raced to the nearest cabin. "Hey, fellas, good news! We're in the wrong camp!"

Well, no sooner had the words left his mouth than Ms. Chalice heard a huge commotion on the other side of the wall. There was shrieking and hooting and howling, which is the kind of thing ghosts do all the time, but it rarely sounded this joyful. A moment later, spirits of all shapes and sizes came streaming out through cracks and creases and water pipes, and they lugged over their bags and got on the ghost bus.

Oh, by the way, there was a ghost bus.

"I hope you enjoy your camp," said the ghost as he climbed aboard the strange hovering vehicle. "Although, personally, I wouldn't be caught dead here."

And just like that, the spectral troopers floated down the road toward Camp Haunt 'n' Howler, a place any ghost would gladly be caught dead in. The bus was almost out of sight when a small, grinning head emerged from one of its windows.

"Oh, one more thing!" the ghost yelled. "Beware the curse of the mountain!"

Then he waved a cheerful goodbye to all the campers, except for Mugman, who had stuffed himself inside his own backpack.

Cuphead rolled his eyes.

"Eh, don't mind that ol' ghost, he's just trying to scare us," Cuphead said, pulling his brother out by the ankles. "I told you before, it's nuthin' but a stupid camp story. Now, come on. If we're gonna fill our whole summer with fun and adventure, we'd better get started!"

Good ol' Cuphead. He always looked on the bright side, even when that side was very hard to find. And in spite of everything, he believed what Elder Kettle had told him—that Camp Hootenholler was the most wonderful camp in the world. He'd just have to look harder, that was all. Still, it would be nice if some kind, helpful person were around to point him in the right direction.

"*Psssssssst*," whispered a voice.

Cuphead turned around. There was no one. Then the hissing noise returned, and this time, he and Mugman followed it to a rundown cabin with its door cracked open just an inch or so. An eye was peeking out at him.

"You there," the eye whispered. "Are the ghosts gone?"

"Yes, they just left," said Cuphead.

Suddenly, the door burst wide open, and the brothers found themselves standing face to face with a very large, very friendly-looking compass.

"Well, that's splendid, just splendid!" the compass said. "Oh, it was terrible having those ghosts around. They kept correcting my grammar! But everything's all right now. Allow me to introduce myself. I am Wrongway North, camp director."

Camp director! thought Cuphead. This changed everything. The camp director would make sure they had the summer of their lives—that's what camp directors were for! Filled with excitement, he quickly summoned the rest of the group. The director gazed out at them, slowly pacing back and forth as if he were conducting an inspection.

"So you're the new arrivals," he bellowed. "My, what a fine-looking bunch! Let me be the first to welcome you to Camp Hootenholler, the most magnificent camp on the face of the earth!"

Now, this was more like it. The campers all wore proud grins on their faces, including Ms. Chalice, even though she couldn't help wondering why the most magnificent camp in the whole wide world would be so short on, well, magnificence.

She glanced at the dilapidated cabins.

"Um, director," she said hesitantly. "Don't get me wrong, you've got a real dandy place here and all, but I was just wonderin'—was there a fire? Or a flood? Or an earthquake?"

"Or a curse?" asked Mugman.

Cuphead looked as if he'd swallowed a sour ball.

"Ix-nay on the urse-cay," he muttered.

But Wrongway just smiled.

"Oh, you mean the appearance of the place." He laughed. "Don't let that fool you. We like our camp to have a rugged, rustic feel. It adds to the adventure! And all those cracks and holes and dents? Why, they give the place character."

"Golly, I've never seen so much character," said Ms. Chalice.

"Exactly!" agreed Wrongway. "Now, follow me, and I'll show you around the camp."

And like a duck before a row of ducklings, he led

53

the procession down the path and into a thick grove of trees.

"Um, Mr. Director," said Tully the turtle. "Isn't the camp over there?"

He was pointing in the opposite direction, toward the place with all the cabins and buildings and camp-like things.

"Oh yes," said Wrongway, scratching his head. "They must've moved it again without telling me."

And he grabbed hold of his large pointy needle (which gives every compass their keen sense of direction) and pointed it the other way. Then, as if nothing had happened, he led the group back to the camp and into the mess hall, which more than lived up to its name.

Cuphead wrinkled his nose.

"Something smells," he mumbled.

Instantly, a large onion burst out of the kitchen. He was on the verge of tears.

"*Uhhhh* . . . good," Cuphead quickly added. "Yep, something sure smells, um, good!"

The onion gave a slight whimper, then lifted the corner of his apron and dabbed at his eyes. Cuphead sincerely hoped he hadn't hurt any feelings, but more than that, he hoped that awful smell wasn't their dinner.

"Campers, this is Ollie Bulb," Wrongway announced. "He's the camp cook."

"It's so nice to meet you all," said Ollie, his voice cracking. "I just know we're going to have the best summer...ev...ev...evvvvERRRRRR!"

And then the tears started to flow like rivers of joy, which was to be expected (onions, as everyone knows, never miss an opportunity for a good cry), and Ollie quickly dashed back into the kitchen.

"And this fellow over here," said Wrongway, pointing to a figure sitting at one of the tables, "is your camp counselor, Cagney Carnation."

Cagney rose to his feet. He was an intimidating sort, a tall, tough-looking flower with shifty eyes and bright-orange petals.

"Now, you listen, and you listen good!" he ordered the group. "We're going to have fun this summer. You hear me? FUN! And anybody who doesn't like it is going to have to answer to me, got it?"

Cuphead gulped. It was the angriest pep talk he'd

ever heard. The truth is, he'd always thought having fun was extremely important, but this was the first time it had seemed like a matter of life and death.

Then, at Wrongway's urging, the campers all took a seat. Ollie reemerged from the kitchen carrying a large silver pot. From it, he dished out portions of a substance Cuphead couldn't quite identify, though he was fairly sure it was some kind of glop. He and Mugman poked at it with their spoons. Even this seemed risky, and eating it was out of the question.

"Well, now that we've had our dinner and taken care of the introductions, I suppose you'd like to see your cabins. Come with me," said Wrongway, and he marched into the kitchen.

Ollie Bulb turned him around.

"Ah, over there now, are they?" said the director, and he reset his needle and walked out the front door.

The group followed him to a long row of wooden lodgings. . . . They were *loaded* with character.

The first one, for example, had a lovely view of the stars, mainly because the roof was missing. The next one wobbled back and forth like a roller coaster. There was one that was ice cold, one that was scorching hot, and one with a faucet that dripped incessantly.

Just what it was dripping, no one could say, but it ate a hole in the bottom of the bathtub.

The good news was that Ms. Chalice's cabin seemed perfectly fine if you didn't count the dust bunnies. Unfortunately, she did count them—there were 214. Also, eleven dust squirrels, two dust cows, and a big furry buffalo named Dusty.

"Oh well, I guess it'll be all right," she said.

There was a snicker from the corner of the room. When the group looked up, they saw a spider. Her web spelled out, *You'll be sorry!*

"Hmmm," mused Wrongway. "Looks like we'll need to find you a broom somewhere. A good sweeping and this place should be right as rain. Well, off we go!"

And then he and Cuphead and Mugman said goodnight and headed down the trail to the next cabin.

"Ah, here we are," said Wrongway, opening the door.

Mugman took a cautious look inside. He half expected to see bats or moths or crabgrass (the crabbiest of all the grasses), but there was none of that. There was a set of bunk beds.

"I call the bottom bunk!" he yelled, and tossed his backpack onto the mattress.

KRRR-AAAAAACK!

In an instant, the top bunk came crashing down, squashing the pack like a grape.

"Or the top bunk," he said. "The top bunk will be fine."

Cuphead paid no attention.

"That's all right by me. I'll just sleep over here."

He walked across the room to a comfortable-looking hammock and prepared to settle in. But before he could plop himself down, the long, skinny cords unraveled and began hissing and slithering across the floor. As Cuphead soon found out, this wasn't a hammock at all, but a collection of slumbering snakes. And since snakes are rarely friendly (and never when they've been rudely awakened), they squirmed out the door without so much as a by-your-leave.

"Well, I'll be off, then. Pleasant dreams," said Wrongway, and he walked outside and began setting mousetraps in front of the cabin.

The brothers watched him.

"Jeepers, that's an awful lotta traps," observed Cuphead. "Do you have a problem with mice?"

"Oh, these aren't for mice," Wrongway told him. "They're for Puncha—"

He stopped abruptly.

"Puncha what?" demanded Mugman.

"Oh, nothing," said Wrongway. "It's just that you can't be too careful out here in the wilderness."

And then he went on with his task, and when he'd finished, he moved silently down the path and did the same thing in front of all the other cabins, because he was a camp director, and that's what camp directors do.

5

WRONGWAY AIN'T RIGHT

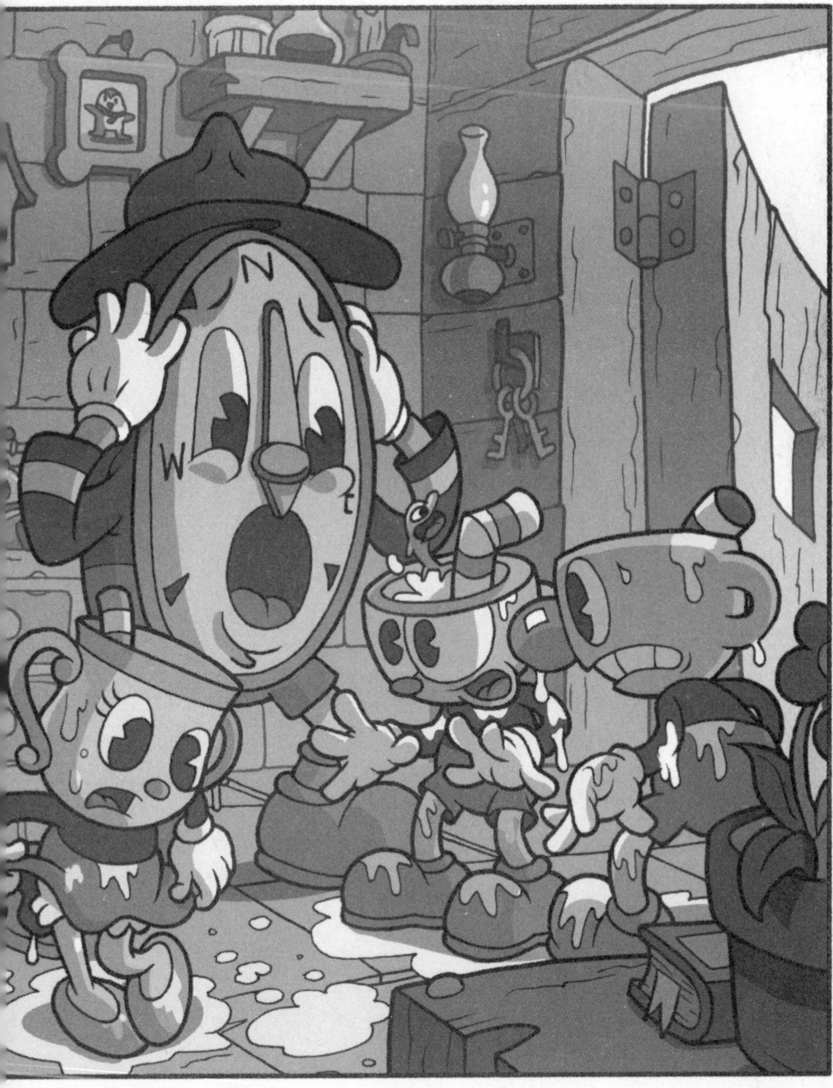
N
W

The next morning, as the orange sun was just peeking over the horizon, a lone figure strutted across the camp yard and assumed his place on a perch. It was a rooster, nature's faithful alarm clock, and he proudly lifted his head, puffed out his chest, and—

"HEY! WAKE UP, YOU LAZY DOLTS!" he said.

This was terribly loud (as roosters tend to be), and Cuphead popped out of the lower bunk like hot bread from a toaster. And a good thing he did, too, because a split second later—

KRRRR-ACK! KLAAAANG! CRRRRAAASH!

Down came Mugman.

"Good morning, Cuphead," he said, yawning sleepily and climbing down from the big pile of bed rubble. "What should we do today?"

"Everything," said Cuphead.

And he meant it. After all, you only get one chance

to have your very first morning at Camp Hootenholler, and he was determined to make the most of it. Filled with excitement, the brothers raced to the sink, pushing and prodding each other to make room for their daily rituals. As usual, Mugman tied a washcloth to a windup toy airplane, which flew into one of his ears, made a long squeegeeing sound, and—*PLOOP!*—popped out the other side. As for Cuphead, he stuffed a bar of soap into his mouth and swished and bubbled and agitated like a pint-size washing machine. Then, when the words *SOAK*, *SPIN*, and *RINSE* had all cycled across his forehead, he gargled, gulped, and wiped his mouth with his sleeve.

There, that was better. And now that the boys were as clean and spiffy as ever they'd been, they leaped into their shoes, burst through the door, and headed out into a world of thrills, adventure, and—

SNAP!

SNAP!

SNAP!

Mousetraps.

"Look, Cuphead," said Mugman. "Wrongway forgot to pick up his traps."

"You don't say," said Cuphead, pulling a metal snapper off the end of his nose.

He was, in fact, covered in traps, and he mumbled several tiny "ouch"es as he plucked them from various appendages. You would've done the same, because mousetraps, it turns out, are very unpleasant objects. Cuphead couldn't imagine why mice were so fond of them.

Just then, Mugman spotted Ms. Chalice making her way up the path. In her hands, she carried a set of thick gray disks that appeared to be made from clay.

"Skeet shooting?" he asked.

Ms. Chalice shook her head.

"Breakfast," she said. "Ollie made pancakes."

She held out one of the frightening flapjacks and let it drop to the ground. It landed like a lead bowling ball.

"Jeepers creepers!" said Mugman.

But Cuphead just shrugged.

"Oh well, I wasn't in the mood for pancakes, anyway," he said. "Besides, who can think about food when we're about to have the best day of our lives?"

They all agreed this was an excellent point, and

despite some very noisy objections from their stomachs, they completely forgot about food and headed off on their quest for the perfect day. They'd only just started when they ran into Tully and Ginger.

"Good morning, Cuphead. Good morning, Mugman. Good morning, Ms. Chalice," said Tully, who was a classmate of the trio and one of the friendliest turtles ever to come out of a shell. "We're off to pick wild blueberries."

Mugman's eyes widened.

"You mean in the woods?" he asked.

Tully nodded.

"Gee whiz, don't you know it's dangerous out there?" said Mugman, shaking his head. "You can never tell when you're going to run into a Punchafink!"

"What's a Punchafink?" asked Ginger.

"I don't know," he said, "but I'm pretty sure it's horrible. Here, you better take one of these for protection."

He handed her a pancake.

Ginger put it in her basket, and the three friends waved goodbye and continued down the path. Suddenly, they heard a loud, shrill noise.

TWEEEEEEEET!

It was Cagney Carnation. He was staring at a clipboard and blowing his whistle like a runaway freight train, because that's what camp counselors do.

"All right, listen up," he told the mob of campers gathered around him. "My job is to take the puny pile of mush that is you and mold it into a lean, mean camping machine. Now, out here in the wilderness, there are two ways to do things: the RIGHT way and the FUN way. We're going to do things the FUN way."

Cuphead perked up his ears. This sounded promising.

"And by FUN, I mean *F-U-N*," Cagney explained. "*F*—fix your own problems. *U*—use your own judgment. *N*—never bother the camp counselor, because I've got enough on my plate already. These new whistles aren't going to break themselves in, you know."

TWEEEET! TWEEEET! he tweeted, because a camp counselor's work is never done.

"But in the end," he continued, "by doing things the FUN way, you'll be learning the most important lesson of all."

"How to make pants out of cheese?" asked Mugman.

"No!" Cagney roared. "Self-reliance!"

"Oh," said Mugman, and he pulled out his very

long *Things to Learn at Camp* list and sadly crossed off *cheese pants*.

Cagney sighed and went on with his address.

"Now, over on the bulletin board, you'll find a paper with all the activities available here at the camp. Well—what are you hangin' around here for?"

TWEEEEEEEEEEEEEET!

He blasted his whistle. Whether this was some kind of starting signal or just routine whistle maintenance, we'll never know, but the campers burst away like a herd of escaping rodeo bulls. Cuphead raced to the bulletin board outside Wrongway's cabin and squeezed his way to the front of the pack. He carefully checked the selections.

"Ah, this is more like it!" he said.

• • • • •

After gathering his supplies, Cuphead followed the path through the woods until he came to a large and beautiful lake. It was exactly the kind of place he was sure he'd find at Camp Hootenholler, and he sat back and soaked up the serenity.

"What a break—the perfect spot for some good old-fashioned fishing," he said, because that was what he'd come here to do.

He held out his pole and tied a stout hook onto the very end of the line. Now all he needed was bait. Well, as anyone who knows anything about fishing will tell you, there's always bait around if you know where to look. And sure enough, not two feet in front of him were several nice plump worms crawling around in the dirt.

"Just what I was looking for," he said.

Unfortunately for Cuphead, worms are a gossipy lot, and they'd all heard about his embarrassing encounter with the earthworm when he'd arrived on the bus. So as soon as they spotted the Wormeater (oh, by the way, they called him the Wormeater), they all retreated into their holes, pulled inside their welcome mats, and rudely slammed their front doors.

Needless to say, this was quite a predicament. Here he was at an absolutely glorious fishing spot without any means of attracting a fish. Anyone else would've given up on the whole thing and gone back to camp— but this was not anyone else, it was Cuphead. And being a resourceful fellow, he simply reached into his pocket and pulled out a length of string. After a few strokes with his trusty drawing pencil, the string had two bright eyes, a crooked little mouth, and, for good measure, a tiny name tag that said *Mr. Wormy*.

"Well, that oughta fool 'em," he said.

Cuphead was almost certain it would. To be honest, fish were not the most intelligent creatures—not the ones he'd met, anyway. They were always ending up on some fishing line because they couldn't help falling for an obvious trick. Poor fish didn't have a clue. It was hard to believe they lived in schools.

Satisfied that this was the perfect solution, he tied the counterfeit worm to his hook and cast the line into the water. There was nothing to do but wait.

RURRRRRRRRRR!

What was that? Cuphead could've sworn he heard something—which was odd, because fish make very little noise.

RURRRRRRRRRR!

And there it was again. Now he was getting annoyed. Whatever was making that sound was going to scare the fish, and he was determined to make it stop. Quickly, he turned his head from side to side, trying to find the source of the disturbance, and then—

RURRRRRRRRRRRRRRRRRRRRR!

He looked down. The sound was coming from his stomach.

"Jumpin' Jehoshaphat!" he said. "I guess I shouldn't have skipped breakfast."

Oh well. There was nothing he could do about it now. Or was there? You see, out of the corner of his eye, Cuphead spotted a very curious thing. It was a positively delicious-looking pie just sitting there on the end of the pier. And when he moved closer, he saw that it was a cherry pie—his favorite—and sticking out of it was a little sign: FREE PI! TASTE GUD. EET IT!

Well, Cuphead didn't have to be told twice. He reached down, picked up the magnificent pastry, and then—

YOINNNNNK!

He was yanked right off the pier. Then down he went, deeper and deeper under the water, pulled by some unknown force. When he finally reached the bottom, he saw that a very large bass was reeling him in with a fishing rod. Well, as you can imagine, this was extremely humiliating. But not nearly as humiliating as when, a second later, a lobster appeared with a camera.

The bass immediately grabbed Cuphead by the ankles, held him upside down, and posed triumphantly for a photo.

CLICK!

Now that the catch was documented, the fish released him (as any true angler would), and Cuphead swam to the surface. A few minutes later, he dragged himself onto the shore, gasping and dripping and wet and cold—but most of all, he was angry. No properly run camp would allow this kind of deviousness on their lake.

What in the world had happened to Hootenholler?

• • • • •

The moment Ms. Chalice looked at the list on the bulletin board, she knew exactly what she wanted to do.

Go canoeing!

After all, what could be better than spending the day peacefully paddling across crystal-clear waters? It was perfect! So quick as a wink, she made her way to the lake and found a row of boats resting on the shore.

"Excuse me," she said. "I'd like to go for a canoe ride. Can any of you take me?"

"Oh yes, I can take you," said a pompous-sounding boat at the front of the line. "My name's Wet Willie, and I'm the finest craft on these waters."

"BAH! Don't listen to Sir Leaks-a-Lot," said the next boat. "I'm Soggy Sue, and I know this lake better than anybody."

"Oh, you're both full of mildew!" yelled a boat named Tipper. "Anyone with eyes can see I'm the best!"

"Don't choose them, they have barnacles!" said Bubbles. "Pick me!"

And then they all started talking at once and saying the most dreadful things about one another, and the situation got very loud and ugly. This was not the peaceful day Ms. Chalice had in mind. But just as she was about to give up on the whole idea, she spotted one little canoe that wasn't making a sound.

"You're awfully quiet," she said. "What's your name?"

"Me?" said the canoe, sounding surprised. "Why, they call me Lucky."

"Then Lucky it is," she said. "Let's go!"

And in two shakes of a duck's tail, they were out on the lake having a wonderful time.

"Ah, this is the life," Ms. Chalice said. "I don't think I'd be enjoying myself nearly as much with those other boats."

"Oh, they're not so bad," said Lucky. "It's just that they haven't been properly maintained lately. None of us have."

"Really? Why not?" asked Ms. Chalice.

Lucky seemed surprised by the question.

"Well, because of all the trouble at the camp, of course."

"What trouble?" said Ms. Chalice.

Now Lucky was really confused.

"You mean you don't know? I thought everyone knew about—"

Just then, a tall spray of water spouted up from the bottom of the boat.

"Oh my goodness," said Lucky.

Ms. Chalice covered it with her hand.

"What's happening?" she asked.

"Um . . . just a little leak," said the canoe. "I'm sure there's nothing to worry about."

And that's when another, taller leak erupted at the opposite end. Ms. Chalice stretched as far as she could reach and blocked it with her other hand.

"Oh boy, is this embarrassing," Lucky said. "I can't believe this is happening again."

"Again?" said Ms. Chalice, who was now plugging a third gusher with her foot. "You mean this has happened before?"

Lucky let out a long sigh.

74

"There's something you should know about me," the boat admitted. "I have a little problem with, um, sinking."

"Sinking?" yelled Ms. Chalice, reaching out with her other foot to block the newest eruption. "Then why do they call you Lucky?"

"Oh, that," said the little canoe. "They're being sarcastic."

"What?" shrieked Ms. Chalice.

"Sarcastic. It's when someone says the opposite of what they really—"

"I know what *sarcastic* means!" she yelled.

But before either of them could say another word, several more leaks appeared, and Ms. Chalice, having run out of ways to block them, just sat there quietly. After a little while, water burst out of both her ears, and then she opened her mouth and spritzed like a decorative fountain as the good ship "Lucky" went down, down, down.

A short time later, a straw broke through the surface of the water and looked around like a periscope. It continued to gaze outward until it reached the shore, and Ms. Chalice climbed out of the lake.

Sopping wet, she sat down and removed a fish from her head. Now she understood what Lucky had meant about the boats not being properly maintained.

But what in the world had happened to Hootenholler?

• • • • •

By the time Mugman reached the area in front of Wrongway's cabin, the crowd of campers was so thick that he had no hope of reading the activities list. He tried pushing his way closer, but since he was confoundingly polite, this got him nowhere.

"Well, this is a problem," he said.

But for every problem, there is a solution, and Mugman calmly walked over to a pair of trees and tied two limbs together. Then, after putting a funnel on top of his head (he always carried a funnel for just such occasions), he pulled back the limbs like the string of a bow and launched himself over the top of the crowd.

SPROI-OI-OI-OINGGGGGG!

In a flash, Mugman plunged funnel-first into the bulletin board and was sticking straight out of it like an arrow.

"Ah, here it is," he said, checking the list. "Archery!"

It was just the kind of camp adventure he'd been waiting for, and the next thing he knew, he was standing on the archery range ready for a day of target shooting. Unfortunately, most of the targets were being used by other archers, but he did manage to find one on the end that he thought would do nicely. It was large and white with a series of concentric circles that led to a bull's-eye in the very center.

Mugman eyed it carefully.

"Piece of cake," he said, and loaded an arrow into the bow.

WHOOOOOOOOSH!

The pointy projectile was off like a missile, and sure enough, it made a direct hit near the exact center of the target. This was real marksmanship! Mugman was ecstatic—that is, until the center moved.

"Now, that's peculiar," he said.

Peculiar was putting it mildly. A bull's-eye simply wandering around willy-nilly was very odd, indeed. And if that weren't bad enough, all the circles surrounding the bull's-eye suddenly got up and moved, as well.

"Hey, stop that!" he shouted. "I have a good mind to speak to someone about this."

Mugman was understandably irritated, but as it turned out, he had bigger troubles. You see, it seems the target he'd selected wasn't a target, after all. It was just a plain white board that proved to be the perfect resting spot for a large swarm of hornets. The fact that they'd arranged themselves into a pattern of target-like circles was an unfortunate coincidence.

"Oh my goodness," said Mugman, realizing his mistake. "You see, I thought—"

But the swarm would have none of it. Hornets, as you know, are angry little creatures who get terribly upset over things like having arrows fired at them, and they were in no mood for excuses. Enraged, they flew off the board and immediately formed a gigantic arrow, which, considering the circumstances, seemed like an appropriate revenge.

The hovering spear soared through the air and headed straight for Mugman.

"AIIIIIIIIIIIIIIIIIGH!" he squealed.

Then he streaked down the trail and made a beeline for the lake. Meanwhile, the hornets made a hornet-line behind him, and they were gaining quickly. Fortunately for Mugman, he reached the pier in the nick of time, raced to the edge, and dived into the water. And since hornets are extremely poor swimmers (mostly because it's almost impossible to find trunks in their size), they gave up the chase and went on their way.

Even so, it was a good long time before Mugman emerged from the lake. But when he was sure the coast was clear, he dragged himself to the shore and collapsed. It was then that he started to wonder how such a thing could happen. After all, no proper camp would let a swarm of hornets go around arranging themselves into elaborate geometric patterns on their archery course. He was thinking it over when he looked up and saw Cuphead and Ms. Chalice standing over him, both dripping wet.

"What in the world has happened to Hooten-holler?" they all said together.

• • • • •

When the trio arrived back at the campground, they found Tully leaning against a post. He looked troubled.

"What's the matter, Tully?" asked Ms. Chalice. "Didn't you find any wild blueberries?"

"Oh yes, we found them," he replied. "It's just that—"

Suddenly, Ginger raced by them screaming at the top of her lungs. She was being chased by a gang of vicious-looking berries.

"Umm... They were wilder than we expected," said the turtle.

Cuphead had heard enough.

"That does it!" he declared, and he, Mugman, and Ms. Chalice stormed into Wrongway's cabin.

"Okay, Wrongway, what's goin' on?" Cuphead said. "We're all having a terrible time! Something has happened to this camp, and we want to know what it is!"

The director gulped loudly and stood up from his desk. He seemed very disturbed and paced nervously around the room muttering something about "that wretched curse" and "those dreadful Punchfinks," though it wasn't entirely clear what he was talking about.

"Say," said Ms. Chalice. "What's the deal with this curse?"

"And what's a Punchafink?" asked Mugman.

But instead of answering them, Wrongway came to a complete stop, grabbed hold of his needle, and turned it in the other direction.

"Curse? Punchafinks?" he said. "I have no idea what you're talking about. This is a wonderful camp, everything is fine, and we're all going to have a magnificent summer. Now, I'm very busy, so you'll have to leave."

"But—" Cuphead said.

"No, no, I'm sorry, there's nothing more to discuss. Thanks for dropping by," Wrongway said, and he herded them out the door.

The three campers stared at one another. Something very strange was happening. They had no idea where to look for answers, but as luck would have it, Ollie Bulb was out for a stroll.

"Hello, Ollie," Cuphead said. "We wondered if you might be able to help us with something."

"Sure, anything for a pal," said Ollie.

"Gee, that's swell of you. You see, we just went in to see Wrongway to complain about—"

"Complain?" Ollie shrieked, and his onion skin turned white as a turnip. "This is about the pancakes, isn't it? I'm trying as hard as I can!"

"No, it's not that—" said Ms. Chalice, but it was too late.

Ollie was already inconsolable, and before they could ask him a single thing, he'd run off into the distance blubbering all the way.

6

A BIG MESS IN THE MESS HALL

Marshmallows, wiener roasts, sis-boom-bah!
Hootenholler, Hootenholler! Rah, rah, RAH!

Cuphead silently mouthed the words as the cheer repeated over and over inside his brain. It was a tasty little chant, and he wanted it to go on and on and then he heard Ms. Chalice.

"Cuphead? Cuphead?" she said. "Are you okay?"

Cuphead slowly opened his eyes. To his great disappointment, he found himself sitting on a long wooden bench in the mess hall. Worse, instead of the marshmallows and wiener roasts he'd been daydreaming about, he was staring at a mysterious substance called "Camper's Surprise."

"What is this?" he inquired.

"There's only one way to find out," said Ms. Chalice, and she bravely reached for her spoon.

"*Ohhhhhhh* no, you're not putting me in there," said

the spoon, leaping up from her place setting. "I want to live. I want to live!"

The utensil then raced across the table and grabbed a dish by the hand.

"Come on, Darla! We're makin' a break for it!"

And just like that, the pair ran away together, as dishes and spoons sometimes do.

Ms. Chalice let out a long, slow whistle.

"I'll say one thing about Camper's Surprise—it sure lives up to its name," she said.

Mugman nodded and laid his head on the table. He was clearly in agony.

Cuphead knew just how he felt. The truth is, he was every bit as hungry as his brother, but the thought of consuming this nightmare-on-a-plate made his stomach do somersaults.

"This stuff isn't fit for a garbage can!" he blurted out.

And the only thing that kept him from blurting a good deal more was that Ms. Chalice was clearing her throat.

"Ahem, *A-HEMMMMMMMM*!"

Now, it seemed to Cuphead this was an abnormally loud *ahem*, which he found very rude—and then he looked up.

Ollie Bulb was standing on the other side of the table.

"Um, like I was saying," he continued, "this stuff isn't fit for a garbage can—it's fit for a KING! Boy oh boy, that Ollie really outdid himself!"

Then, as casually as he possibly could, he glanced across the table.

"Oh, hi, Ollie! I didn't see you standing there. Why, your footsteps must be as light and airy as those golden, flaky biscuits of yours. Tell me, how do you put together such a sumptuous spread?"

The cook rubbed a hand across his chin.

"So you really like the food?" he said suspiciously.

"And how!" fibbed Cuphead.

Ollie crossed his arms.

"So why aren't you eating it?"

Oh dear. This was the question Cuphead had been dreading. He pondered it for a moment, scratched his head, and gulped.

"I, uh, I was just about to," he said, and with a quivering hand, he forced a bite past two of the most unwilling lips you'll ever see.

"*Mmmmm,*" he groaned.

All things considered, it was a persuasive

performance, and it would've been even more so if his face hadn't turned green.

Ollie, however, was unconvinced. He just stood there eyeing the little green camper and looking for the slightest hint of deceit. But after a moment or two, the tension subsided, and he broke into a grin.

"Well, if you think that's good, just wait until you try the dessert," he said proudly. "I've made something extra special!"

And with that, the onion happily turned on his heels and hurried off to the kitchen.

"*Blechhhhhh!*" said Cuphead.

And then his tongue popped out like a hideaway ironing board. Ms. Chalice didn't like the looks of it. For one thing, there was a little sign that said, THIS PROPERTY IS CONDEMNED, and for another, his taste buds were loading their things into a tiny moving van.

"Yikes!" she said.

"Don't worry, Cuphead," Mugman told him. "I'll bet Ollie's dessert will get that horrible taste out of your mouth."

Cuphead's face slowly rotated until his gaze locked onto his brother.

"Dessert? Are you out of your mind? I'm lucky I survived the meal!"

In fact, Cuphead could think of no fate worse than having to try another of Ollie's calamitous concoctions. Dessert? Why, the very idea! So no, he would not be consuming another morsel, thank you very much, and that was all there was to it. And that's exactly how it would've stayed if Tully, who was sitting at the next table, hadn't intervened.

Tully, as you know, was a very intelligent turtle who knew a great deal about life and the path to happiness. He was always the first to lend a hand whenever anyone was in need, and he freely shared his insights with friends and strangers alike.

And while he was never pushy with his philosophies, on this particular occasion, he felt Cuphead might benefit from another point of view.

"You know, Cuphead, in situations like this," he said, "I find it's best to keep an open mind. There's an old turtle saying: *If you never come out of your shell, you'll miss all the world has to offer.*"

The serene little turtle craned his neck as far as he could and took a long, exuberant whiff of the air. The scent coming from Ollie's kitchen wafted around him like magical fingers, and for a brief moment, he hovered blissfully above the ground.

"Everyone has a talent, Cuphead," said Tully. "Even Ollie Bulb."

Cautiously, Cuphead, Mugman, and Ms. Chalice synchronized their sniffers and took a long whiff of the aroma that had lifted Tully from the floor. It was spectacular! It was as if cinnamon and caramel and toffee and cream had formed a band, and now everyone's nostrils were doing the boogie-woogie.

"Wow! There's a party in my nose, and man, is it swingin'!" said Ms. Chalice.

This was amazing. Was it really possible that Ollie was a wizard with sweets? The three friends immediately tied their napkins around their necks and held their knives and forks in the ready position. All they had to do now was wait.

And wait.

And wait.

And wait.

Cuphead looked at the clock on the wall. It seemed to have stopped moving or, at the very least, was running so slowly that eons passed between the *ticks* and the *tocks*. It was unbearable.

"What's taking so long?" he demanded.

"That's what I want to know!" said Ms. Chalice.

"Will this torture never end?" screamed Mugman.

Finally, Cuphead could stand it no longer, and he climbed up on top of the table.

"Great gallopin' gollywompers!" he bellowed. "Enough is enough! Why do they serve us terrible food when we don't want it but make us wait forever for the good stuff?"

Just then, a barrage of garbanzo beans splattered against Cuphead's cheek. A look of horror crossed his face as someone—he didn't know who—called out that dreaded phrase that has struck fear in the hearts of cafeteria workers since the beginning of time.

"Food fight!"

"Oh no," said Cuphead.

In an instant, the entire hall was in chaos. Tables were toppled, benches were battered, and the air was thick with campground cuisine. Dishes flew like flying saucers. Saucers flew like flying dishes. Eggs were scrambled, salads were tossed, and a fleet of gravy boats slowly sank into the chicken noodle sea. But if you think that was the whole of it, you are very much mistaken. Because in every part of the room, campers were launching legumes, propelling parsnips, catapulting cucumbers, and chucking chestnuts. And when a submarine sandwich managed to torpedo Mugman's ankles, he responded with a banana bombardment that would go down in the annals of Hootenholler lore.

Because at that very moment, Ollie Bulb was at last departing the kitchen with his long-awaited dessert. Caught in the crossfire, he stepped to his left, where his foot landed on an unfortunately placed banana peel. Well, the next thing he knew, his legs went topsy-turvy, the dessert flew into the air, and before anyone could do anything about it—

PLOP!

It came down on top of his head.

"How...how...how could you?!" he said. "Just look what you've done!"

And then the tears burst from his eyes like water from an open fire hydrant.

It was a sorrowful sight, and everyone in the very messy mess hall fell completely silent. Then they turned and looked at the door.

Wrongway was standing there.

Cuphead wasn't sure what was going to happen

next. He thought there might be yelling or scolding or any number of gruesome punishments, and all of them would be deserved. But, in the end, there was none of that. There was only Wrongway staring at the room with a look of deep and profound sadness.

"This used to be quite a place, you know," he said softly. "Yes, it was quite a place."

7

HOOTENHOLLER GETS A TUNE-UP

The campers slowly poured out of the hall and into the grounds. Cuphead had a bad feeling in the pit of his stomach, partly because he was thinking about Ollie and Wrongway, and partly because one does not try the Camper's Surprise without consequences. He felt terrible about what had happened, and he wasn't alone. They were all ashamed of what they'd done and haunted by the ache in Wrongway's voice.

This used to be quite a place, you know, he had told them.

It was a pain Cuphead knew very well. He had been raised on Elder Kettle's memories of the old Hootenholler, the greatest camp in the world. It was a destination he'd dreamed of all his life. But now it was time to face the truth. As bad as the food fight was, it didn't make much difference at Camp Hootenholler. It just made the mess hall look like the rest of the place.

The camp of his dreams was a run-down shadow of what it once had been, and that was a terrible shame.

"Oh well, there'll be other summers," said Ginger, putting into words what everyone was thinking.

And in a great silent migration, all the campers turned and began their sad, slow trek back to the row of dilapidated cabins.

Well, not *all* the campers. There was one standing alone in the center of the camp yard, not going anywhere. It was Ms. Chalice, and when she finally opened her mouth to speak, out came the last thing anyone would have expected.

"Horsefeathers," she said.

Yes, she said *that*. Well, as you can imagine, every slumping head suddenly popped right up and looked at her. After all, you don't call *horsefeathers* on something without a very good reason, and no one knew this better than Ms. Chalice. So, like scattered tacks drawn to a magnet, the departing campers swiftly turned themselves around and headed back to the center of the camp yard.

Cuphead gave his friend a very serious look.

"Explain yourself," he said.

"I'd be delighted," said Ms. Chalice, and she

stepped forward and gazed at the group huddled around her. "Now, we all think Hootenholler is a lousy camp, right?"

"Right!" said the campers.

"And we all think we got a raw deal by coming here, right?"

"Right!" they said again.

"And we all think our summer is ruined, right?"

"Right!" they shouted, and their heads bobbed up and down like a row of seesawing pump handles.

"Horsefeathers!" said Ms. Chalice.

An audible gasp rose up from the crowd. This was not the kind of language one generally heard on a warm summer evening in Mother Nature's backyard. But Ms. Chalice was just getting started.

"Take a look around," she told them. "What do you see? Some broken windows? Some loose boards?"

"Some carnivorous plants," said Mugman, pulling his head out of the jaws of an oversize tulip.

"Yes, those, too," Ms. Chalice agreed. "This camp certainly has its problems. But it's also got fresh air and sunshine and all the wild adventures you could ever ask for. And you know what else it's got? It's got us."

The campers all looked at one another. They

weren't sure where Ms. Chalice was going with this, but they liked the way it sounded.

"Don't you see?" she told them. "We can still have the summer we've always wanted. Hootenholler isn't such a bad place. It just needs some sprucing up. And if we all work together, we can make it better than ever!"

There was a sudden, very enthusiastic burst of applause. But it wasn't coming from the campers.

It was coming from Quint.

The bus driver had been listening from the shadows. Now he moved into the light and strolled to the center of the crowd.

"Oh, goody, the cleanup crew is here," he said, and not in a nice way. "Let me tell you sumpthin'. You won't even make a dent in this place before it's time to pack up and go home. There's only one way to fix what's goin' on around here, and that's...eh, forget it!"

He took the last bite out of an apple and tossed the core on the ground.

"You wanna clean sumpthin' up? Start with that. Have fun wastin' your summer, chumps!"

And then he laughed a fiendish laugh (you know,

the kind that sounds like a hyena with a bad chest cold) and went on his way.

Oooooooh, that Quint! Cuphead's blood was boiling! The driver had been annoying on the bus, but here in the campground he was just plain mean. But what made Cuphead angriest of all was that he had a point.

He looked around at the camp. Then he looked at Ms. Chalice.

"How in the world are we going to fix all this?" he said.

Ms. Chalice flashed a neon smile.

"Easy," she told him. "We'll just give the place a tune-up!"

And without another word, she put two fingers in her mouth and whistled. Right on cue, the Four Mel Arrangement popped out of a tree stump and went straight into a catchy little ditty that went something like this:

Bom, bom, bom, bom—
WHEN *you're* POUTIN' *'cause your* PLACE *is a*
   MESS—
Bom, bom, bom, bom—

AND *you're* DOUBTIN' *it'll be a* SUCCESS—

Bom, bom, bom, bom—

Don't STAND *there* HONKIN' *like a* GAGGLE *of*
   GEESE—

Just PUT AWAY *the* GLOOM *and grab some*
   EL-BOW GREASE!

ELBOW *grease,* ELBOW *grease!*

Turns a MESS *into a* MAS-TER-PIECE—

YOU *won't* NEED *a lot of* EX-*per*-TISE—

When you GET *the* JOINT *to* JUMP*in' with some*
   EL-BOW *grease!*

BOM-*bom*-BOM-*bom!*

BOM-*bom*-BOM-*bom!*

GRAB *a* BROOM *and* SWEEP *your* WORRIES
   away—

Bom, bom, bom, bom—

GET *to* SCRUBBIN', *it'll* WORK OUT *okay*—

Bom, bom, bom, bom—

FIX *your* TROUBLES *with a* HAMMER *and*
   NAILS—

When you INCREASE *your* ELBOW GREASE, *it*
   NEV-*er fails!*

ELBOW *grease,* ELBOW *grease!*

Turns a MESS *into a* MAS-TER-PIECE—

102

YOU *won't* NEED *a lot of* EX-*per*-TISE—
When you GET *the* JOINT *to* JUMP*in' with some*
EL-BOW *grease!*

Well, as anyone who has ever had a big job to do will tell you, the right song can make a world of difference. There's something about music that just makes the work fly by in a flash. That's certainly what happened at the camp that day, and if you'd been there, you would've been absolutely amazed. You see, as the Mels crooned along (in perfect four-part harmony, of course), Hootenholler began transforming in a way that can only be described as some sort of miracle. Everywhere you looked, campers were hammering and sawing, dusting and scrubbing, painting and plastering, and giving the whole place the kind of industrial-strength makeover usually reserved for movie stars. Naturally, it was only a matter of time before the rhythm spread throughout the camp—there were daffodils tooting their trumpets, rattlesnakes shaking their maracas, bluebells ringing, songbirds singing, and a pair of dancing grizzlies who stumbled across some sawdust and broke into their ol' soft-shoe routine.

As for our trio of friends, they were as caught up in the melodious mojo as anyone. Mugman, for example, was chopping wood when he suddenly found himself playing the logs like a xylophone. It was the same with Cuphead. Out of the blue, he grabbed a rake, stood it upright, and strummed the thing like a bass fiddle. And when Ms. Chalice heard the zippy chorus, she immediately dropped what she was doing (which unfortunately was the dishes) and performed a spirited drum solo on a garbage can.

Yes, it was quite a spectacle, and there were lots of other things happening, too—but it's probably best to let the Mels tell you about that.

Bom, bom, bom, bom—
WANT *to* TRAV-*el down a* CLEAN-*er* PATH?
Bom, bom, bom, bom—
GIVE *that* HIKING *trail a* BUB-BLE *bath—*
Bom, bom, bom, bom—
DUST *those* BUN-*nies out of* EV-*ery* ROOM—
And FRESH-*en up that* SKUNK-*weed with some*
    SWEET PERFUME!
ELBOW *grease,* ELBOW *grease!*
Turns a MESS *into a* MAS-TER-PIECE—

YOU *won't* NEED *a lot of* EX-*per*-TISE—
When you GET *the* JOINT *to* JUMP*in' with some*
   EL-BOW *grease!*
OHHHHHHHHHH!
SICK *of* SLOPP-*i-ness? Well,* HERE'S *the*
   CURE—
GIVE *that* MA-*ple tree a* MAN-*i-cure*—
DRESS *those* DAIS-*ies in some* HAUTE
   COUTURE—
To MAKE *a* DUMP *a* DOO-*zy all it* TAKES IS
   YOUR—
ELBOW *grease!* ELBOW *grease!*
ON *sale* NOW *for* TWO BITS *apiece!*
When you USE *it* FUN *will* NE-VER CEASE!
So JUST *put on that* GEN-U-INE—
When you WANT *the* PLACE *to* REALLY *shine*—
Just PUT ON *that* EL-BOW GREEEEEEASE!
ELBOW GREASE!

When the number ended, the whole camp started clapping and hooting and cheering, but the Mels paid no attention. They simply plopped themselves into the nearest mop bucket and floated away on some large soapy bubbles.

The great ones always know how to make an exit.

And as the campers stood there, waving goodbye, Mugman joined Cuphead and Ms. Chalice at the front of the pack.

"Cuphead?" he asked. "What did Quint mean when he said—"

"*Shhhhhhhh!*" Cuphead shushed him. "It's time."

And sure enough, at that very moment, the door to the director's cabin creaked open and out came Wrongway. When he looked down the path, he saw a row of bright faces staring at him—and then his eyes widened.

Wrongway quickly grabbed hold of his needle and pointed it in the other direction. Just like that, his downturned mouth curved into a smile.

"It's . . . it's unbelievable," he said. "Why, it's just how it used to be! What a marvelous surprise. You've done a fine job, campers. No, you've done better than fine—you've done a Hootenholler job!"

And feeling happier than he had in quite some time, he wandered down the path for a thorough inspection. Cuphead walked along beside him but stopped when he saw Quint leaning against a post.

"So, what do you think of the place now?" he said proudly.

At first, Quint didn't say anything. Then he scrunched up his mouth and raised an eyebrow.

"Not bad for a bunch of chumps," he said. "But good luck keepin' it like this."

Then he laughed that long, wicked laugh of his, and though Cuphead didn't know why, he had the strangest feeling that Hootenholler's troubles were not yet over.

In fact, they were just beginning.

8

MARSHMALLOWS & MYSTERIES

That night, the entire group made their way to a clearing in the woods for one of Hootenholler's most cherished traditions: the campfire gathering. Everyone was very excited about being there, but they were even more excited about something else.

Marshmallows!

Oh, it may seem like a small thing to you, but compared to Ollie's cooking, toasted marshmallows were a royal feast. Of course, the trick was in the toasting, and Cuphead—though he'd be the last one to brag about it—was something of an expert. He carefully placed the sugary tidbit onto the end of a long stick and held it out over the flames. By slowly rotating the magical morsel around and around, he gave it a light, even, crispy brown coat. This one was turning out to be a real work of art, and he was very pleased—until he saw Ms. Chalice.

Her stick had *five* marshmallows all lined up in a row.

"I see you're still doing yours one at a time. That's cute," she told him.

Cuphead scowled at her. Then, almost as if they had one head between them, they both turned and looked at Mugman. He was holding a full tree branch over the fire. Dangling from it were dozens of sweet, gooey puffballs.

"Amateurs," he said.

And then they all laughed and settled in for a night of delicious treats—and deliciously spine-tingling tales.

Now, you do know about campfire tales, don't you? Those terrifying, ghostly, ghoulish stories guaranteed to scare the living daylights out of the bravest of marshmallow munchers? Why, of course you do. They've been around forever. All right, not forever, but at least since the time of the prehistoric cave-campers, who undoubtedly needed something to talk about as they sat there, roasting rocks or twigs or whatever it was people snacked on before the invention of food.

Yes, there's nothing like a bloodcurdling yarn just

before bedtime to ensure that everyone has pleasant dreams that night.

Well...dreams, anyway.

So when their bellies were full and their fingers were as sticky as warm cotton candy, the campers huddled close together, listening to the crackle of the fire and the howl of the wind and the low, lingering voices eerily weaving their tales of dread.

"It was a night just like this one," said Tully, setting the mood. "And a group of campers who, if not for the hand of fate, could've easily been you or me, were sitting around an open fire discussing the meaning of existence. Suddenly, a gigantic chicken with huge red eyes and razor-sharp talons burst out of the woods. And he looked at the campers and said, 'I crossed the road. But why? Why?'"

The campers waited. Then waited some more.

"Is that it?" grumbled Canteen Hughes.

"Yes," said Tully, and he smiled serenely.

Everyone looked at everyone else, and then they all looked at the turtle.

"Gee, that was, um, swell, Tully," said Cuphead. "But the story was supposed to be scary."

"In the dark of night, there's nothing scarier than an unanswered question," Tully said.

The whole group got chills. And after they'd talked it over and taken into consideration the philosophical implications, they all agreed that very few things in this world are as scary as a giant chicken.

Next, Ginger rose to her feet. She told them about a girl who had been sent to bed without any supper and had the most wonderful dream that night.

"But when she woke up the next day, she found that she hadn't been eating a giant marshmallow at all," she whispered. "It was her own pillow!"

The campers all gasped. Mugman was nearly frantic.

"This wouldn't happen if they just made pillows out of marshmallows in the first place!" he shouted, and everyone agreed this was a very good idea.

There were a couple of other stories—one about pirates and one about a ghostly squirrel searching for her acorn—and then the group got deathly quiet, as groups around campfires tend to do. That's when Cagney Carnation made his way to the circle.

"So, telling scary stories, eh?" he said. "Well, I've got a story so scary you won't be able to sleep again until you're back home safe in your beds. And the worst part is—it's true!"

The campers' eyes grew until they were the size of billiard balls. You could hardly blame them for being nervous—the only thing that made campfire stories bearable was knowing that they weren't real. And now, to hear that one of them actually could've happened—well, this changed everything.

Cagney pushed aside a couple of campers and squeezed into the circle. The firelight flickered across his face like a tiny thunderstorm.

"What I'm about to tell you didn't happen in some faraway place. It happened right here at this very camp," he said in a deep, ominous voice. "In fact, it's still happening—and you're all part of the story!"

The campers froze in mid-gawk.

"The thing about camps," he began, "is that some of 'em are good, some of 'em are bad, and a very few—like this one—*are cursed!*"

At that moment, all the marshmallows hanging from Mugman's tree branch melted into the shapes of little ghosts. The gooey ghouls let out a hideous laugh.

"Aaaugh!" he cried, and dropped the branch into the fire, but no one paid the slightest attention.

They were too busy listening to Cagney.

"It all started a long, long time ago," the counselor told them. "You see, back then, Hootenholler was just about the swellest place on the map. Yessiree, this camp was a real humdinger—and then *they* came...."

"They?" asked Cuphead.

"The Punchafinks!"

"PUNCHAFINKS!" the campers shrieked, and they turned very pale and trembled.

"That's right, Punchafinks," said Cagney. "They started their own camp on the other side of the lake, see? But because they were Punchafinks, they were loud and rowdy and ruined everything they touched. And if that weren't bad enough—they woke up Glumstone!"

The counselor waited for the shock of this announcement to wear off. He didn't have to wait long.

"Um," said Ms. Chalice, "who's Glumstone?"

"Who's Glumstone?" he roared in disbelief. "Why, he's the big cheese around here, that's who! Glumstone the Giant is a huge and powerful mountain, not to mention the meanest ol' hill you're ever likely to meet. And when those Punchafinks woke him up in the middle of a fifty-year nap, you better believe he was plenty sore! He shook the ground and sent giant boulders flying through the air! But here's the tricky part—because he was a mountain, every camper just looked like an ant to him. And since he couldn't tell a Hootenholler from a Punchafink, he decided to put a curse on both camps."

"The curse of the mountain!" gasped Mugman.

"Exactly. The curse said that the best of the two camps could stay and live in harmony with nature. But the worst camp would be destroyed!"

This, as you can imagine, was disturbing news. But Cuphead just crossed his arms.

"If this curse is so terrible, then why are there still two camps?" he asked suspiciously.

A small grin wriggled across Cagney's face.

"Well, Mr. Smarty Pants, I'll tell you," he said. "You see, ol' Glumstone fell back asleep before he could decide which camp was best. And what do you think those lousy, no-good Punchafinks did then? They sabotaged us, that's what! Between their midnight raids and their dirty tricks, they've spent years trying to turn Hootenholler into a wreck. Because they know that one day, the mountain's gonna wake up again, and when he does, he'll pick out the worst camp and—*WHAM!*—smash it to smithereens! So now you know why every Hootenholler camper has to be on constant lookout for Punchafinks."

"But what does a Punchafink look like?" asked Ginger.

Cagney leaned in close and his voice got very low.

"Like somethin' out of a nightmare," he said. "They're ten feet tall with gigantic horns and long, twisted faces—and they breathe fire! Oh, a Punchafink's like nuthin' you've ever seen before. They can sneak up on you anywhere at anytime, but I'm pretty sure we're safe here as long as nobody makes a—"

"AAAAAAAARRRRRRGGGGGGGH!"

Suddenly, there was a terrifying screech, and a horrible creature leaped out of the bushes! It was ten feet tall with a twisted face and gigantic horns on each side of its head! And when a stream of fire burst out of its wretched mouth, the campers screamed at the top of their lungs—and that's when they saw Cagney fall over backward.

"*Ha-ha-ha-ha-ha-ha-ha-ha-ha-ha-ha!*" he wailed. "You should see the looks on your faces! 'Run! Run! It's a Punchafink!' *Ha-ha-ha-ha-ha!*"

Cuphead was furious. He walked over to the

massive intruder and pulled away the large, twisted mask. It was Ollie Bulb walking on a pair of stilts and holding a little torch.

"We gotcha! We gotcha good!" Ollie snorted, and he laughed and laughed until he was crying.

Cuphead turned around and stormed back to the still-shivering group of campers.

"I told you the curse was a big joke!" he said. "They just wanted to scare us!"

"Oh, they definitely wanted to scare us—and they did it," said Canteen Hughes. "But I'm not sure you're right about the curse. My grandfather was at Camp Hootenholler years ago, and he said giant boulders really did fall from the sky!"

Oh dear. This wasn't what the campers hoped to hear at all. No one wanted boulders raining down on them. It sounded awfully painful and couldn't possibly be good for their umbrellas. Fortunately, Tully chimed in with a helpful suggestion.

"It seems to me there's only one thing to do," he said. "We've just got to work extra hard to make Hootenholler the best camp it can be!"

Everyone thought this was a fine idea—well, not everyone.

"Sure, that's one way to do it—if you wanna be a bunch of chumps," said Quint, stepping out from behind an oak tree. "Don't you see? You don't need to make this camp better, you just gotta make their camp worse. Hit 'em before they hit you, got it?"

Then he grinned an oily grin that made him look like some kind of sinister troll.

Cuphead frowned. He didn't know if there really was such a thing as a Punchafink, but if they existed, they certainly hadn't done anything to him. And besides, the last thing he wanted was advice from Quint.

"Forget it," he said. "We're not gonna cause trouble for anybody else because of a dumb ol' story about some phony-baloney curse. If we run into any campers, then we'll be good neighbors—because that's the Hootenholler way!"

Of course, all the campers agreed completely, but Quint just shook his head and rolled his beady little eyes.

"Suit yourself." He sighed. "But don't say I didn't warn you."

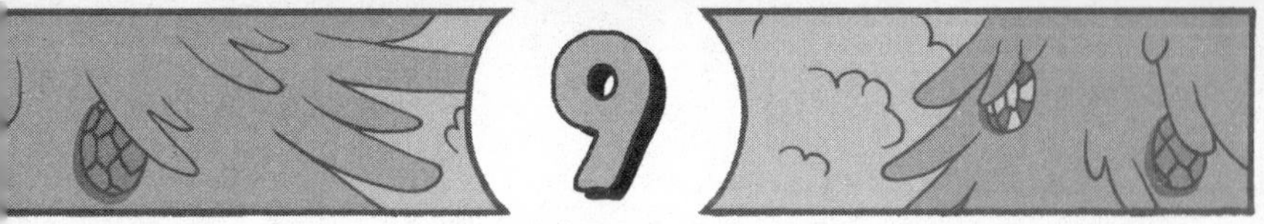

9

IT'S A PUNCHAFINK!

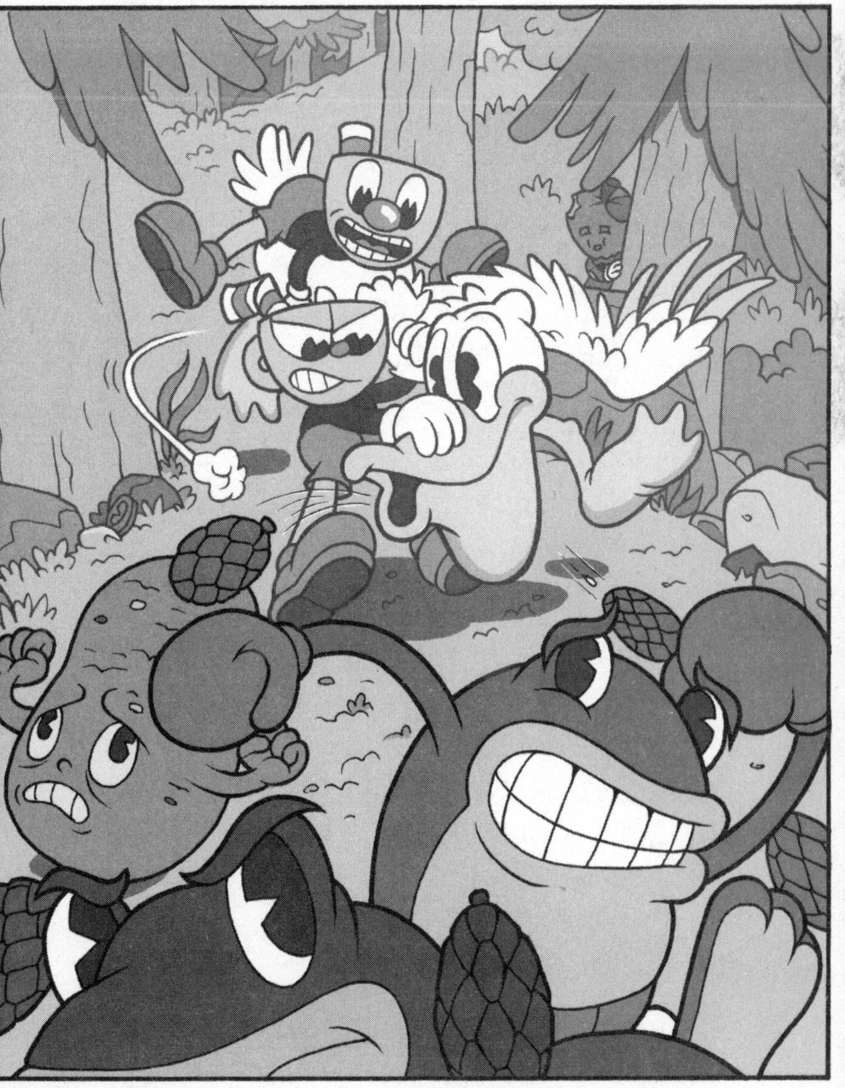

The campers all slept under the stars that night. Of course, technically, they always slept under the stars (you should look up sometime—the sky is literally jam-packed with those things), but in this case, they were outdoors with no roof between them and the great, twinkling canopy above, and that made it special. And when Cuphead woke up early and eager the next morning, he knew just what he wanted to do.

"Let's take a nature hike!" he said, and everyone enthusiastically sprung up from their sleeping bags and threw their shoes at him.

"The sun's not even up yet," grumbled Ginger. "Go back to sleep!"

Well, if you know anything about Cuphead, you know that sleeping was the last thing on his mind. This was a time for adventure, and he wasn't going to waste a single minute. So what if some of the other campers didn't share his excitement? He could always count on his two loyal companions.

"Sheesh," groaned Ms. Chalice. "Do we really have to do this?"

She was dragging a still-sleeping Mugman behind her.

"Come on, it'll be fun!" Cuphead said cheerfully. "I'll pack a lunch."

So he rustled up some marshmallow sandwiches, marshmallow salad, pickled marshmallows, and a canteen of turnip juice (which didn't taste too bad as long as you put some marshmallows in it), and they were on their way.

As the trio hiked down the silent trail, the sun peeked over the horizon and winked at them. Mugman stretched and yawned.

"Good morning," he said. "Where am I and why am I here?"

"We're on a nature hike, and you're here to read the field guide," Cuphead told his brother.

Well, as you can imagine, Mugman was very excited. He was never without his trusty field guide, a handy booklet filled with interesting facts about nature and the various things in it. He pulled it out of his pocket and began browsing the pages.

"Oh, here's something," he said. "It's a guide to different kinds of plants. For example, do you know what that is?"

"It's a tree," said Ms. Chalice, because it looked like a tree.

"Ah, but what kind of tree?" Mugman asked. "You see, different trees have different characteristics."

Hmmmmm... This sounded like it was a challenge. Ms. Chalice was intrigued. After all, there's nothing she enjoyed more than a test of skills, so she moved closer to the specimen in question and gave it a thorough examination. It was large and thick with a tangle of branches and a bushy array of leaves.

"Is it a birch?" she asked.

Mugman checked his list.

"No, it's not a birch."

"An ash?" she said.

He shook his head.

"Well, what is it? A mulberry? A locust? A catalpa?"

"A Roger," said the tree.

Ms. Chalice took a rapid step backward.

"Excuse me?" she asked.

"That's my name—Roger," said the tree. "Not that you bothered to ask."

He let out a long, annoyed sigh.

"Oh, I didn't mean to disturb you," Ms. Chalice told him. "We were just trying to figure out what kind of tree you are."

"And you think you can tell that just by looking, do you?" he said.

"Well—"

"Because it seems to me that if you really wanted to know what kind of tree I am, you'd have taken the time to get to know me. Or does that little book tell you that I'm an avid reader who enjoys rainy days, birdwatching, and doing the Sunday crossword?"

He seemed very irritated.

"Oh no, it's not like that. We weren't trying to find out about you personally," Ms. Chalice explained. "We just wanted to identify you as—"

"An oak tree," said Cuphead, who knew about these things.

"Yes, as an oak tree," she said.

"Oh, I see," huffed Roger. "What you're saying is you weren't looking at me, you were looking at an oak tree. Because all oak trees are the same, right? If you've seen one of us, you've seen us all! It's not as if we have feelings or hopes or dreams or anything to share with the world. Except oxygen, of course—you're welcome, by the way. No, you've made yourself perfectly clear. There's nothing special about old Roger. I'm just a big pile of wood to you."

"No, that's not what I meant!" Ms. Chalice assured him, but Roger was in no mood to listen.

"How would you like it if I only thought of you as a category?" he said. "I'd just open up my handy-dandy field guide and say, 'Oh, look, there's a camper. But there's nothing interesting about her because she's exactly like that camper, and that other camper, and those four campers over there by the lake, and so on.' It gets a little monotonous, doesn't it?"

"Did you say there were four campers over by the lake?" asked Cuphead.

Roger held out his branch and pointed. Sure enough, four campers were coming ashore on a raft. Cuphead's face broke into a wide grin.

"Well, would you look at that! We should go introduce ourselves."

"Oh, sure, now you want to introduce yourselves," said Roger.

Of course, you couldn't blame them for being excited. One of the very best things about spending a summer at camp was having the chance to make new friends. So, without a moment's delay, the three of them hurried down to the water's edge.

"Hello there," called Cuphead. "We saw you coming across the lake on your raft. She's a real beaut!"

"Thanks, we built it ourselves," said a girl wearing a very smart little pirate hat.

Cuphead held out his hand.

"I'm Cuphead, and this here is Mugman and Ms. Chalice."

"I'm Cora," said the girl, squeezing his hand like it was an uncracked walnut. "And that's Sal Spudder, and those two are Ribby and Croaks."

She pointed to two large frogs and a muscular potato. They were dragging the raft onto the shore. Cuphead waved but the group paid no attention.

"Jeepers, I'd sure like to be able to build a raft like that," he said.

"Oh, this is nuthin'," Cora told him. "We're learning how to build all kinds of swell stuff at camp."

Cuphead couldn't help feeling a little envious.

"Is your camp around here?" asked Ms. Chalice.

"Yes, it's on the other side of the lake," said Cora. "We're from Camp Punchafink."

Well, well, well, the infamous Camp Punchafink! Cuphead had a million questions, but before he could say a word—

"PUNCH-A-FINNNNNNNNKS!" shrieked Mugman.

And then his arm shot up like a warning sign pointing out danger. Cuphead immediately threw a hand over his brother's mouth.

"You'll have to forgive him," he said. "He's never met a Punchafink before. You see, we're from Camp Hootenholler."

Ribby and Croaks both turned and looked at him. Sal Spudder growled.

"Oh, Hootenholler," said Cora, and there was a nervous sound in her voice. "How do you, um, like it over there?"

"It's aces," said Cuphead. "Just a swell place."

Ribby and Croaks snickered to themselves.

"If you like garbage," Sal muttered.

Cuphead frowned and narrowed his eyes. Then he remembered his pledge to be a good neighbor.

"I'll admit it had some problems when we arrived,

but we've got it all fixed up now. It's better than ever!" he said.

"Oh, I'm sure you did the best you could," Cora told him. "Still, it seems like a waste of time, considering..."

"What do you mean, 'considering?'" Ms. Chalice said.

"Well, considering it's going to be destroyed. Nuthin' personal. It's not your fault the camp is cursed."

"You take that back!" Ms. Chalice yelled, and Cuphead held her by the collar while she punched blindly at thin air.

"Look, there's no curse," Cuphead said. "And even if there was, what makes you think your camp wouldn't be the one destroyed?"

All the Punchafinks laughed out loud.

"Because Camp Punchafink is the best. We've always been the best, and we always will be," Cora explained. "Our grounds aren't a disaster. Our cabins aren't held together with bubble gum and string. And while the Punchafinks are standing here with a raft we built ourselves, the Hootenhollers are standing here with—"

She looked at Ms. Chalice, who was still swinging at invisible invaders.

"That," she said.

The rest of the Punchafinks strolled over and joined Cora.

"Just wondering, does your director still get lost every time he walks out of a room?" Ribby cackled.

"No! Not every time!" yelled Mugman.

The argument could have gone on and on, but Cuphead had heard enough. Clearly Punchafinks were every bit as bad as Elder Kettle had described them, and there was no point in continuing the discussion.

"Let's get outta here," he told his friends.

So the three of them turned around and began walking back up the trail.

"Have a good time at Camp Hurtin' Holler!" Sal Spudder called after them.

"Oh, we will. Have fun at Camp Bunch-a-Stink!" said Cuphead.

And that's when the rock bonked him in the back of the head.

Cuphead swiveled around with a gleam of pure vengeance in his eyes. But the Punchafinks just stood there whistling a little tune, their hands cradled innocently behind them.

"All right," he snarled. "One of you is a lousy, no-good rock flinger!"

"Oh, you're wrong," said Cora, flashing a playful grin. "We're all lousy, no-good rock flingers."

And without another word, the four of them began to pummel the Hootenhollers with a shower of stones.

"Take cover!" Cuphead yelled, and a moment later they were hunkering down in a clump of trees.

"What'll we do now?" asked Ms. Chalice.

Cuphead was wondering the same thing himself. He quickly scanned the area.

"What's that?" he asked, pointing to an odd-looking bird who happened to land nearby.

Mugman checked his field guide.

"Pelican," he said.

Well, that was all Cuphead needed to hear. He quickly snatched the bird off the ground and held her under his arm like a set of bagpipes.

"Load her up," he said.

"With what?" asked Ms. Chalice, and it was a very good question. It wasn't as if pelicans came with their own ammunition.

The three of them were stumped. But just when it looked like all hope was lost, Roger gave his leaves a furious shake. Out fell hundreds of acorns.

"Nothing to see here, just Roger being incredibly

helpful," said the oak tree. "I don't suppose it mentions that about me in your field guide?"

"I'll pencil it in!" cried Ms. Chalice, and she grabbed an armload of acorns and dumped them into the bulging pouch on the pelican's bill.

While Cuphead held the bird, Mugman clutched her feet and took careful aim. The brothers each took a deep breath.

"Now!" Cuphead said.

Suddenly, out came a rapid-fire stream of woodland projectiles. The rock-throwing Punchafinks were pelted over and over, until finally, finding themselves defenseless against the relentless acorn assault, they retreated back to the safety of their raft.

"Hooray!" the friends cheered as they watched the enemy sail away.

"That'll learn 'em!" said Ms. Chalice.

Naturally, the three of them thanked Roger many times, and the pelican just as many. Then, giddy with the elation of victory, they turned around and made their way back to camp.

"We have met the Punchafinks in battle!" Cuphead announced proudly when they returned to the group. "And we have won!"

The campers let out a rousing cheer, and they wanted to know all about the Punchafinks and what had happened. The trio told them the whole story, and when they were done, the group begged them to tell it again.

It was a great day for Hootenholler!

But even in the midst of celebration, there was one figure who looked anything but pleased. Wrongway had an expression of dread like they'd never seen before.

"Oh goodness. Oh dear, dear me," he muttered. "I do hope that's the end of it."

Cuphead didn't know what the director was so worried about. Maybe his needle was pointing in the wrong direction again? After all, this was good news, and good news was something to celebrate.

And that's exactly what the Hootenhollers did.

10

THE MIDNIGHT RAID

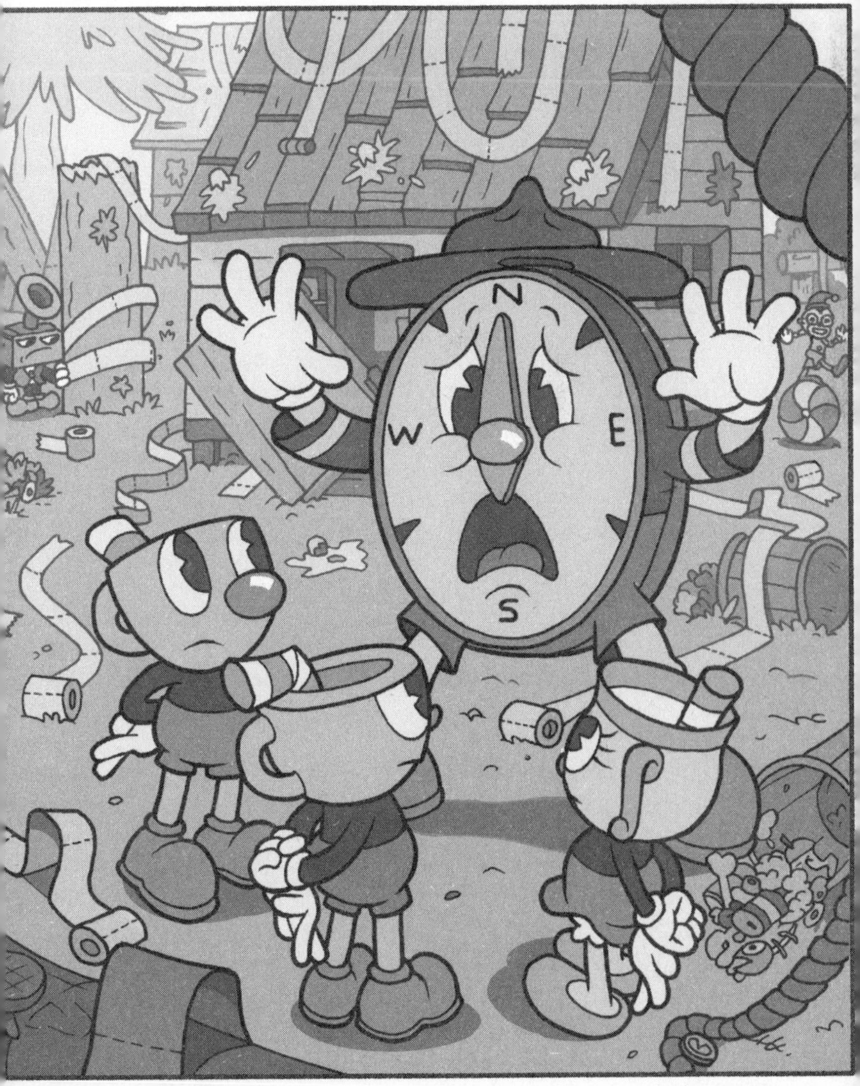
N
W
E
S

Cuphead had very pleasant dreams that night. For the first time since they arrived, he dreamed of the friendly bear and of sipping sweet pineapple juice and of skiing effortlessly across the lake behind a motor boat. But even good dreams must end, and all too soon came the first glimmer of daylight, and with it, the rooster's melodious call—

"Jumpin' jiminy!" the early bird screeched. "What in tarnation went on here last night?"

Cuphead and Mugman leaped from their bunks and rushed out of the cabin. They found the others waiting for them.

"Look at this place!" said Ms. Chalice.

It was not a pretty sight. Strewn across the camp were old tin cans, heaps of litter, and every kind of muck. Flowers were trampled, signs were torn down, and the place looked nearly as miserable as it had on the day they arrived.

"What could've caused this? Was there a tornado last night?" asked Ginger.

"This was no tornado," said Canteen Hughes, giving the grounds a long, deliberate stare. "It was the curse!"

The curse! Of course, what else could it have been? Everyone agreed there was really no other explanation, and they all broke out in a terrible case of goose pimples (except for the geese, who broke out in people pimples), as frightened campers tend to do.

Cuphead believed it was a curse, as well—but not the kind inflicted by some fabled mountain. This calamity had a much more malevolent source.

"Punchafinks!" he growled.

It all made perfect sense. The Punchafinks, angry about their humiliation at the lake, raided the camp in the middle of the night. It was just the kind of destructive act Cagney had warned them about in his campfire tale.

"Punchafinks?" said Ginger. "But I thought you said they'd be too scared to show up here."

"Well, I uh—" Cuphead stammered.

"Yeah, you said you'd taught them a lesson they'd never forget!" said Canteen Hughes.

Mugman glanced at the camp.

"I guess they forgot," he said.

Well, suffice it to say the campers were not pleased. The air was filled with loud, angry voices, and an army of accusing fingers sprung to attention and pointed at Cuphead. Then a tall, slim figure pushed his way through the crowd.

"You!" snapped Cagney, giving Cuphead a venomous glare. "You just had to go and stir things up with the Punchafinks, didn't you? Well, look around, smart guy! I hope you're happy—you've ruined everyone's summer!"

And before Cuphead could even begin to explain, the cantankerous carnation wheeled about and stormed down the path.

The crowd moved in closer.

"Jeepers, it's not my fault," Cuphead told them. "Can I help it if Punchafinks are too stubborn to know when they're licked? And remember, they attacked us—we were only defending ourselves. Besides, what happened at the lake doesn't matter now. What matters is what happened here last night!"

Now, furious as they were, the campers had to admit these were valid points. Slowly, they turned and gazed at their beloved Hootenholler. It was a real mess.

"Cuphead's right!" yelled Ms. Chalice, moving to the center of the pack. "The Punchafinks did this! Are we just gonna stand here and let 'em get away with it?"

"No!" roared the crowd, and then it grew louder than ever, chanting things like "Avenge Hootenholler!" and "Punish the Punchafinks!" and "Wallop the Wormeater!" (though that last one might've just been the earthworms), and they pumped their fists and practiced the most terrifying scowls.

"I say we go find those Punchafinks and settle this the Hootenholler way!" bellowed Cuphead, and the camp responded with a rousing cheer. "All right, then, we'll need about a dozen pelicans, a cartload of acorns, and—"

"Excuse me," said a quiet voice at the rear of the crowd. "Do you mind if I say something?"

The voice was whisper soft and could easily have been lost in the turmoil. But there was something about its kindness and sincerity that made the group stop what they were doing and listen.

"Now, I know this looks bad, and I don't blame

anyone for being upset," said Tully. "But the fact is, no one saw what happened. So even though we might have our suspicions—and have very good reasons for having them—we don't actually know that it was the Punchfinks. Please understand, I'm not saying it wasn't them, but I do think we should be careful. I mean, do we really want to retaliate against someone who might turn out to be completely innocent?"

Well, as you can imagine, this led to a good deal of grumbling and shrugging and pacing the ground. After all, there's nothing an angry crowd dislikes more than working itself into a good furor only to have someone come along and bring reasonableness into the picture. The truth is, no one was quite sure what to think. Then, as the sun climbed higher in the sky, Wrongway's long shadow fell upon the group.

"This is a very wise young turtle," he told the crowd. "We can all learn from his example. Because whether it was the Punchafinks or whether it wasn't, nothing good can come from continuing this ridiculous feud. It will only bring more destruction and more unhappiness. So as your director, I'm asking you— let it end here. There will be no war with Camp Punchafink. Is that clear?"

"Yes, Director," the campers replied.

Wrongway turned and looked at the gathering's ringleaders.

"And we're going to forget all about this, right?"

"Absolutely," said Cuphead.

"Positively," said Ms. Chalice.

"I've forgotten already," Mugman told him.

The director took a long, probing look at their faces and—after scratching his chin and wrinkling his forehead—decided he was satisfied. Of course, if he'd taken a peek behind their backs and discovered the three sets of secretly crossed fingers, he might have felt differently, but there's no use dwelling on that now.

"Very good," he said. "Now, let's put this unfortunate event behind us and get on with having a great summer. That's the Hootenholler way!"

The campers nodded their heads and dutifully retreated to their cabins. Cuphead started back, as well, but on the way, he ran into an obstacle.

"I hate to say I told you so—but I told you so," the obstacle gloated.

"Leave me alone, Quint," said Cuphead.

But Quint did not leave him alone. He followed Cuphead all the way back to the cabin, repeatedly reminding him of how right he'd been about the Punchafinks.

"I told you if you didn't hit them, they were going to hit you. And look what happened," he said.

For someone who hated to say I told you so, Quint said it an awful lot.

Cuphead sighed and reached for the doorknob. But for some reason—he wasn't sure why—he hesitated.

"We don't even know that it was the Punchafinks," he said.

Quint's eyes nearly rolled out of his head.

"Oh, come on!" he groaned. "This is the most Punchafinky thing I've ever seen! Take a look at this place! You don't seriously think anyone else would've done this, do ya?"

And there was the rub. The truth of the matter was, Cuphead didn't think it was anyone else, and if anyone but Quint were asking, he would've told them so. But he wasn't about to give the smirking bus driver the satisfaction.

"Gee whillikers, will you lay off?" Cuphead said. "Wrongway told us to forget about it, and he knows best. So you can just drop it because I'm not gonna do anything to the Punchafinks."

A grimace crossed Quint's face, but it quickly turned into that horrible smile of his, the one that made the world a little less sunny.

"Sure, just leave 'em alone, Wrongway knows best," he gabbed. "And next time, instead of wreckin' up the place, they'll probably bring tea and cookies."

"Next time?" asked Cuphead. "Why would there be a next time?"

Quint raised a worrisome eyebrow, then turned to leave.

"There's something you should know about Punchafinks, kid," he said, walking away. "They always come back."

11

OOTENHOLLER'S REVENGE

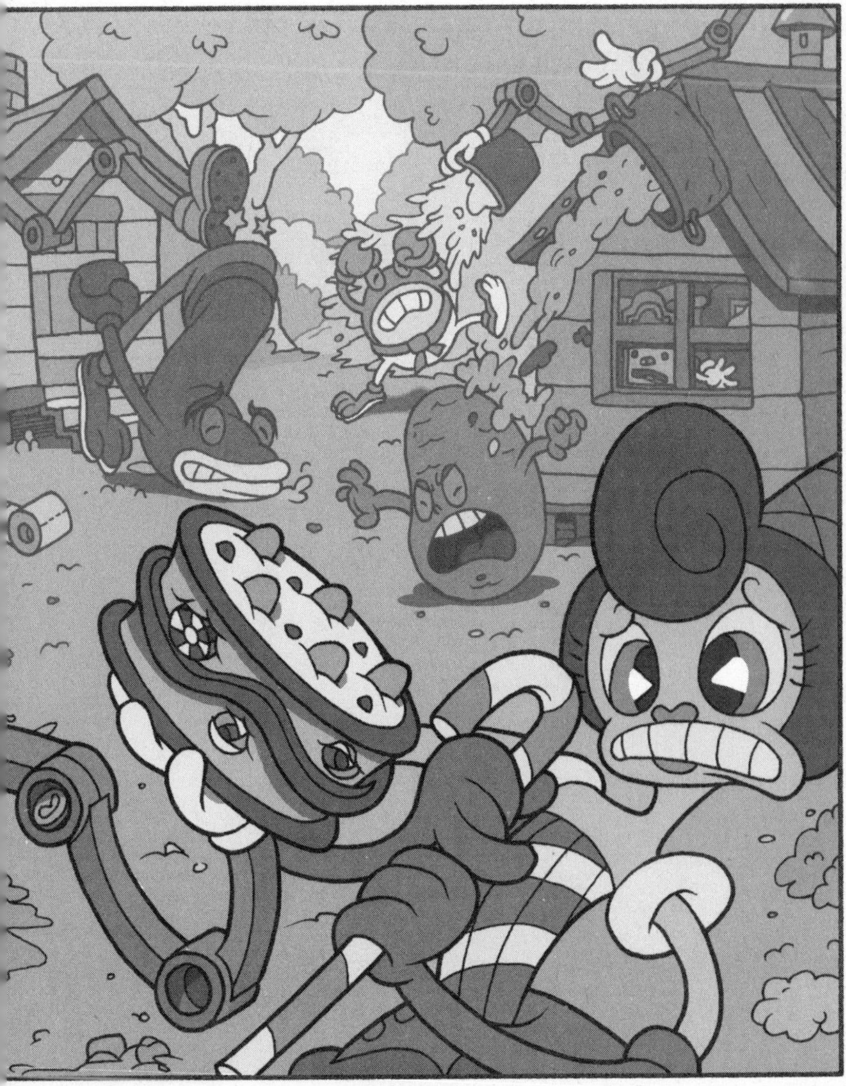

That night, Cuphead couldn't sleep.

It wasn't because the bunk above his bed—*Screeeeeek! Screeeeeek!*—was rocking back and forth like a ship in a storm. And it wasn't because the weeping willow outside his window—*Boooo hoo hoo hoo! Booooooooo hoo hoo hoo hoo!*—was a good bit weepier than usual. It wasn't even because the playing cards had gotten out of the box again, and the one-eyed jack and joker were arguing over which of them was wilder.

No, it was because Quint's words were echoing over and over inside his head.

They always come back. . . . They always come back. . . . They always come back. . . .

It was a disturbing thought. Not that he believed it, of course—not for a minute. This was Quint, after all, and he was hardly a reliable source. Still, Cuphead couldn't help wondering if every crackle and creak

147

might be the pirate girl or the potato back for another nefarious mission. He felt silly lying there in the dark imagining all kinds of ridiculous things, and he was determined to—

WOOOO-OOOO-OOOSH!

What was that?! Cuphead heard a mysterious whooshing noise coming from outside the cabin. It sounded just like the wind—but was it the wind? Or was it some Puncha-fiendish plot to create a hurricane using a giant electric fan? He couldn't rule it out, not with those Punchafinks! *Ooh*, it would be just like them to try and blow Camp Hootenholler completely off the map, and after Wrongway had been willing to let bygones be bygones, too! Why, he had a good mind to—

No! No! No! What was he doing? These were perfectly ordinary nighttime noises and nothing more. It was foolish to lose sleep over it. And even if the Punchafinks were at that very moment concocting sinister schemes inside their factory of evil—and they almost certainly were—it was none of his business. He'd told Wrongway he would let it go, and let it go he would.

Cuphead fluffed his pillow, then pinched the cords on his eyelids and rolled down a pair of tiny shades.

"*Pssssssst*," said a voice in the darkness.

"Oh no," said Cuphead, trying to ignore it.

"*PSSSSSSSSST!*" the voice said again.

"Ouch!" yelped Cuphead, because that's what happens when a very tiny figure pokes you with an even tinier pitchfork.

He opened his eyes. There, hovering just above his throbbing left shoulder, was a very, very small cup that, if it weren't for the horns and the pointy tail, could've been his twin.

"What do you want?" said Cuphead, frowning at the purveyor of all his worst instincts.

"I want ya to get outta this bed and go give them Punchafinks the ol' what for," his bad side said. "C'mon, ya know ya want to!"

The truth is, Cuphead did want to get even. It's why he'd crossed his fingers when Wrongway asked him to forget all about it. He knew he couldn't forget—not after seeing the Punchafinks up close. They were like insects that bored into your brain and haunted your every thought.

"No, Cuphead, don't do it!" said a figure above his right shoulder.

Cuphead rolled over. This one also looked like him, but he had wings and a little halo above his straw.

"Oh no, not you, too," he groaned. "Why can't you leave me alone?"

"Because I'm your conscience, Cuphead," the hovering cup said. "And I will not let that pint-size scoundrel lead you astray!"

"Hey, who you callin' pint-size?" asked Bad Cuphead.

"If the itsy-bitsy shoe fits—" said the good one, and then the two of them began squabbling like rival brothers reaching for the last cupcake.

Cuphead covered his ears.

"Please, just let me go to sleep," he begged.

"Sleep? How can ya sleep knowin' them Punchafinks are out there laughin' at ya?" said the one with the horns. "If I was you, I'd—"

"Don't listen to him, Cuphead!" the other one yelled. "Listen to Wrongway. He'll steer you in the right direction!"

"That don't even make sense," said the bad one.

"*You* don't make sense!" the good one retorted, and that started the argument all over again.

Finally, Cuphead could stand it no longer.

"Look, I'm not gonna do anything!" he told

them. "I'm gonna stay right here and go to sleep, and hopefully that'll be the end of it."

"Good for you, Cuphead," his better self sang. "You've made the right decision. And I, for one, think it shows real character. Virtue is its own reward, after all, and you have proven yourself to be a good neighbor and a credit to . . ." and he went on and on and on and likely would have gone on a good bit longer if—*BONK!*—a rock hadn't conked him in the noggin.

"Ha-ha-ha-ha-ha-ha-ha!" howled Bad Cuphead.

"Ow!" yelled the victim. "That hurt!"

"Don't I know it," said Cuphead, and he explained how one of the Punchafinks had done the very same thing to him during their encounter at the lake. Bad Cuphead grinned.

"And then you grabbed a pelican and did what comes natural—ya got even," he said proudly. "Yep, nuttin' feels better than sweet—"

BONK!

And that's when a rock knocked him off Cuphead's shoulder.

"You know, he's right. That did feel good," said Good Cuphead.

A miserable groan rose up from the floor.

"And you'd be doin' it—*ugg*—for the honor—*oww*—of Hootenholler," Bad Cuphead moaned.

The honor of Hootenholler? Cuphead hadn't thought about it that way before. This changed everything. He wouldn't be doing it for himself, but for Elder Kettle and Sawbuck and Dumpy and Scooter and all those proud Hootenhollers who had come before him. It wasn't revenge; it was a sacred duty! Sure, Wrongway had been against it, but there was always the chance his needle was out of alignment. Why, one good adjustment, and he could have a complete change of heart.

"I'll do it!" said Cuphead, waving the little figures away. "I'll defend the honor of Hootenholler, even if I have to do it alone!"

But since defending honor is even better as a shared experience—especially when it's dark and scary outside—he decided to wake up Mugman.

• • • • •

"Do you think it'll work?" whispered Mugman.

"Of course it'll work," Cuphead whispered back. "At least, I hope so. I'd hate to think we did all this work for nuthin'."

"It's not for nuthin'; it's for the honor of

Hootenholler," said Ms. Chalice, who, to no one's surprise, had joined them on their adventure.

Not that the brothers had any choice in the matter—she'd been there waiting for them when they'd sneaked out of their cabin.

"What took you so long?" she'd asked impatiently. "I've got a hankerin' for some prankerin'."

Pranks, you see, were one of Ms. Chalice's many specialties, and she relished the idea of getting back at the Punchafinks. It wasn't until Cuphead had explained that getting even was their sacred duty that the mission took on a higher purpose.

Now here they were, waiting in the darkness outside the horrible Camp Punchafink. Of course, you couldn't tell it was horrible just by looking—what with its well-kept cabins, immaculate grounds, and fancy hand-carved statues—but it was horrible, all right. Cuphead was sure of it. After all, these were Punchafinks, and a camp was only as good as its campers.

Fortunately, they'd found a very clever hiding place. They were crouched behind a row of neatly groomed hedges that were thick enough to provide excellent concealment yet close enough to give them a front-row seat. And that seat was about to come in awfully handy, because an orange glow had just begun to form on the horizon.

"It won't be long now," said Cuphead.

And sure enough, right on cue, the most highfalutin rooster any of them had ever seen marched out to a tall perch, pulled out a trumpet, and played the morning reveille. Well, it wasn't exactly reveille, it was more like a reveille-esque boogie-woogie number with a jumpin', jivin' beat that set a lively tone for the entire day.

"Show-off," said Ms. Chalice.

But that was only the beginning. Because not long after the wake-up call, a door to one of the cabins burst open, and who should walk out but Sal Spudder. The potato stretched and took a deep breath, clearly enjoying the morning—and that's when a bucket of gruel fell onto his head. It was sticky, slimy, offensive gruel, and Sal raised the most dreadful fuss. Naturally, this caused doors to open all over the campground, and each time a camper stepped out, they ended up wearing a bucket of breakfast like a hat. When the final bucket dropped, it pulled a long rope, causing a row of garbage cans to tip over like dominoes. The last can activated a spring under a porch, sending a small girl (the fact that it was Cora was a delightful coincidence) somersaulting through the air, then landing on an inclined plank that—*SPLAT!*—sent a buttercream-frosted cake into the waiting face of Camp Director Baroness Von Bon Bon.

As the stunned baroness stood there wiping frosting out of her eyes, a large banner ascended the flagpole.

GREETINGS FROM CAMP HOOTENHOLLER.
HAVE A SWELL DAY!

Now, if anyone noticed the shrubbery in the corner laughing hysterically at these events, they didn't bother to mention it. Then again, they likely had other things on their minds. As for Cuphead, Ms. Chalice, and Mugman, their work here was done. Stealthily, they sneaked away from the befuddled Punchafinks and made the happy trek back to camp.

The sun was high in the sky when they arrived, and they couldn't wait to tell their camp mates what had happened. But no sooner had they stepped onto the grounds than they heard a thunderous voice.

"Wrongway!"

Baroness Von Bon Bon—still covered in buttercream—was storming down the path.

"Baroness!" said Wrongway, rushing to meet her. "Oh, goodness me, what happened?"

"I'll tell you what happened!" cried the baroness, shaking an angry finger in the air. "Someone attacked my beautiful camp!"

Cuphead, Mugman, and Ms. Chalice collectively gulped.

Well, for the next several minutes, the tall, impeccably dressed visitor detailed exactly what had transpired that morning. Meanwhile, Wrongway paced nervously back and forth muttering things like "oh dear" and "good heavens" and "my, my, my" in the most sympathetic tone possible.

And when he was quite sure she was finished, he politely leaned toward her and said, "My dear baroness, I do feel awful about what happened to you. But what has that got to do with us?"

The baroness narrowed her eyes and unrolled a large banner.

GREETINGS FROM CAMP HOOTENHOLLER, it said.

"Oh, mercy!" cried Wrongway.

Slowly, his face sunk into a look of deep anguish, and he apologized many, many times. This, he assured her, was not the Hootenholler way, and he pledged to never let it happen again.

"I don't want your apologies or your promises,

Wrongway," said the baroness. "I want the perpetrators punished!"

Wrongway had been afraid she'd say that. He was, after all, a kindhearted camp director, and punishments were such an unpleasant task.

"Yes, of course," he told her, then turned to address the assembled campers. "I have just received some very distressing news about an attack on Camp Punchafink. It involved buckets of gruel, several garbage cans, and a buttercream-frosted cake!"

A giggle rolled through the crowd.

"It is no laughing matter! I want to know who is responsible for this," he said, and he held up the banner wishing the Punchafinks a swell day.

The giggle turned into a snicker. Wrongway was very embarrassed.

"Come, now, the baroness is waiting. Who did this?" he asked.

But when he scanned the faces of the campers, all he saw were angelic expressions of innocence.

"This is a waste of time!" the baroness shouted. "If the perpetrators won't come forward, I demand you punish the entire camp!"

"But, Baroness—" said Wrongway.

"You heard me!"

Poor Wrongway. The baroness had put him in a very awkward position. He didn't want to be unfair, but at the same time, the camp could not afford any more trouble with the Punchafinks.

"Very well." He sighed. "Campers, since no one has taken responsibility, you are all immediately confined to—"

"Wait," said Cuphead.

Every head turned and looked at him.

"Yes, Cuphead?" said Wrongway.

Cuphead swallowed the large lump in his throat and took a reluctant step forward.

"It's all my fault," he confessed. "I take full responsibility. I'm the one who disobeyed you, and I'm the one who should be punished."

Wrongway looked as disappointed as they had ever seen him. He glanced at the baroness, then turned his eyes back to Cuphead.

"You leave me no choice, Cuphead," he said. "I hereby sentence you to the Cabin of Shame."

12

THE MOWER, THE MERRIER

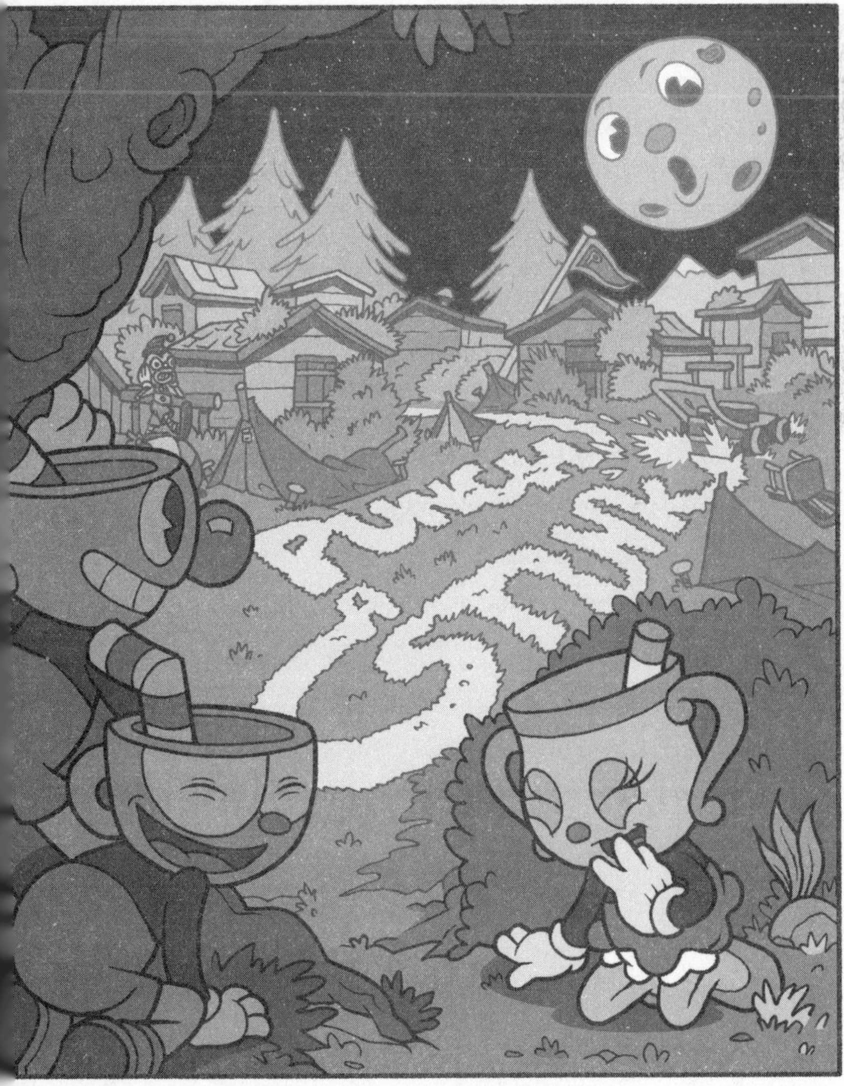

In a ceremony befitting the seriousness of the situation, Cagney and Quint each took Cuphead by an arm and marched him through the crowd of campers.

"Step aside, bad cup walkin'," declared Cagney. "*Baaaaad* cup walkin'."

It was humiliating. Then again, if you've been condemned to something called the Cabin of Shame, you can hardly expect a ticker-tape parade.

"Well, here it is," said Quint. "Ain't she a beaut?"

She was not a beaut.

The Cabin of Shame wasn't so much a cabin as a maximum-security toolshed. It was taller than it was wide, and the one window in the structure was lined with steel bars. There were signs posted all around it reading, SHHHHH! SHAMING IN PROGRESS and DO NOT FEED THE PRISONER and DON'T LET THIS HAPPEN TO YOU! It was a thoroughly shameful experience.

Cagney opened the padlocked door. In the center of it was an odd hole with a little target drawn around the outside.

"What's that for?" asked Cuphead.

"Apples," Cagney told him.

"I get apples?"

"No!" the counselor grunted. "You stick your head through the hole, and we throw apples at you. It's a camp tradition."

Well, Cuphead did not like the sound of that at all. But if it was a camp tradition, he supposed it was his duty to uphold it. So with a long, sad sigh, he stepped through the doorway and, a moment later, heard the horrible *CLICK* of the padlock.

•　•　•　•　•

"Pssssssst! Pssssssssst!"

Cuphead would have known that *Pssssssst* anywhere. It was Ms. Chalice! He immediately rushed to the hole in the door and stuck his head through it.

A plump red projectile splattered against his face.

"You know you don't *have* to throw apples," he told her.

Ms. Chalice looked around cautiously to see if anyone was listening.

"That wasn't an apple; it was a tomato," she whispered. "I thought it would be softer."

"Gee, thanks," he grumbled. Then another one smacked him in the kisser.

"Anyhoo," said Ms. Chalice, warming up her throwing arm, "I've been talking with Mugman about how we're going to bust you outta there."

Cuphead's eyes widened.

"That's terrific! But I wouldn't want you to get into trouble."

She waved away his concern.

"Don't worry about us. We can handle it," she assured him. "Anyway, I'm not gonna let my pal take a bum rap after what those Punchafinks did to our camp. It was a matter of honor!"

"The honor of Hootenholler!" said Cuphead.

"Exactly," said Ms. Chalice.

And she nailed him with another tomato.

"You could miss once in a while, you know," he said.

Ms. Chalice checked again for prying ears.

"Listen, we're going to spring you tonight. So wait for our signal," she whispered.

"I will!" said Cuphead, and he watched her turn and stroll across the camp yard.

• • • • •

It was a cold night, and Cuphead shivered on the bare floor of the Cabin of Shame. He didn't know what time it was, but it seemed very late, and he'd almost decided his friends weren't coming, after all.

Then a sleek yellow paper airplane gracefully sailed through the bars of the window and landed beside him. He eagerly unfolded the note.

The door is unlocked. Get out now! it said.

Well, Cuphead did not need to be told twice. He leaped up off the floor, swung open the door, and—

"WHOAAAAAAAAA!"

—plunged into thin air. You see, the little cabin was no longer sitting at ground level. Someone had placed a jack underneath it and boosted the shed to a stratospheric height. Cuphead fell through the darkness until he—*PLOP!*—splashed down in a large vat of what he instantly recognized as maple syrup. When he climbed out, he was covered in a thick, sticky gunk.

And that's when he saw the balloon.

There was nothing especially interesting about it, just a plain, simple red balloon floating through the air with a box tied to it. And when that box was directly above Cuphead, it opened, showering him in a blizzard of fluffy white feathers.

"Ha-ha-ha-ha-ha-ha-ha!"

Cuphead heard laughter coming from the other side of the camp yard. By the light of the moon, he could make out Cora and her two frog henchmen in near hysterics over the sight of him.

"Well, will you look at that?" the pirate girl shrieked. "We opened the coop and out came a big chicken!"

Cuphead did not react. He just stood up straight and tried to make himself look as dignified as possible.

"You realize this means war," he said.

· · · · ·

Cuphead spent most of the next day plucking himself.

"Still in a *fowl* mood?" asked Ms. Chalice.

"Very funny," he told her. "You know, this would've never happened if you'd busted me out like we planned."

"We told you, we couldn't," said Mugman. "Cagney was keeping an eye on us to make sure we didn't try anything. Also, he tied a bell to me."

He jingled the little silver bell hanging from his straw.

"You could've just taken the bell off," Cuphead reminded him.

"I like the way it tinkles," his brother said, and he gave it a musical shake.

It was early evening, and the three of them were spending it hiking through the woods. Cuphead, you see, was once again a camper in good standing. After the feathering incident, Wrongway decided he'd been shamed enough, and he canceled any further punishment.

"I hope you've learned your lesson," the director had said as he led the sticky jailbird back to his usual cabin.

"Don't worry, I have," Cuphead assured him.

"Good," said Wrongway. "Now, don't let me catch you pulling another stunt like the one that got you into trouble."

"Oh, I won't," said Cuphead.

Wrongway nodded and turned to leave.

"Oh, and Cuphead," he said, "don't let the Punchafinks catch you, either."

Cuphead grinned from ear to ear.

Now, sitting here in the woods with his two best friends in the world, he thought about Wrongway and how Hootenholler was very lucky to have him. Oh, he might make a wrong turn now and then, but all in all he was a very fine director. Certainly better than that Baroness Von Bon Bon!

"If I never see that baroness again, it'll be too soon," Cuphead said.

"But isn't that her down there?" asked Ms. Chalice.

Cuphead looked over the edge of the precipice they were walking along.

"Oh, so it is," he said.

You see, the route the campers had taken on their hike through the woods just happened to bring them to a ledge directly above Camp Punchafink. If one were of a particularly suspicious nature, they might conclude Cuphead had planned it that way—but of course, that would be wild speculation.

"Do you hear something?" Mugman asked his companions. "It sounds like—"

"A lawn mower!" yelled Ms. Chalice, and she pointed to a runaway machine currently plowing its way through the camp.

As the three watched from above, the mower cut down the decorative hedges, turned a hand-carved statue into a pile of splinters, and sent a host of Punchafinks diving for cover.

"Oh, dear me," said Cuphead, taking a casual glance at the chaos below. "I wonder how that could've happened? Well, no use hanging around here. It's time we headed back."

And so the three of them quickly picked up their gear and started down the trail. Still, Cuphead couldn't resist one last glance over his shoulder.

Behind him, he saw that the mower had finally come to a stop—but not before it had clipped *PUNCH-A-STINK* in giant letters across the camp yard.

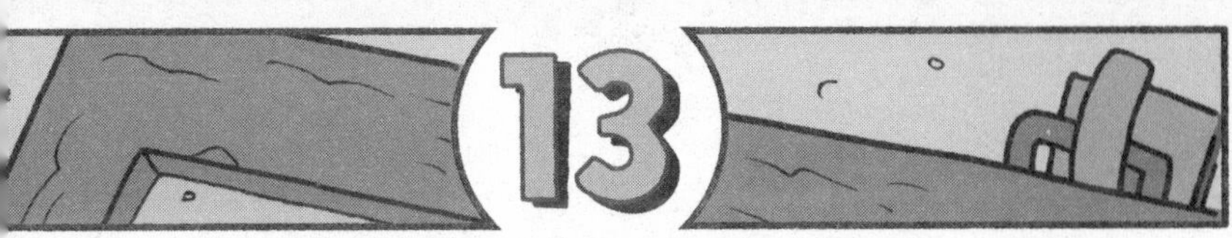

13

THIS MEANS WAR!

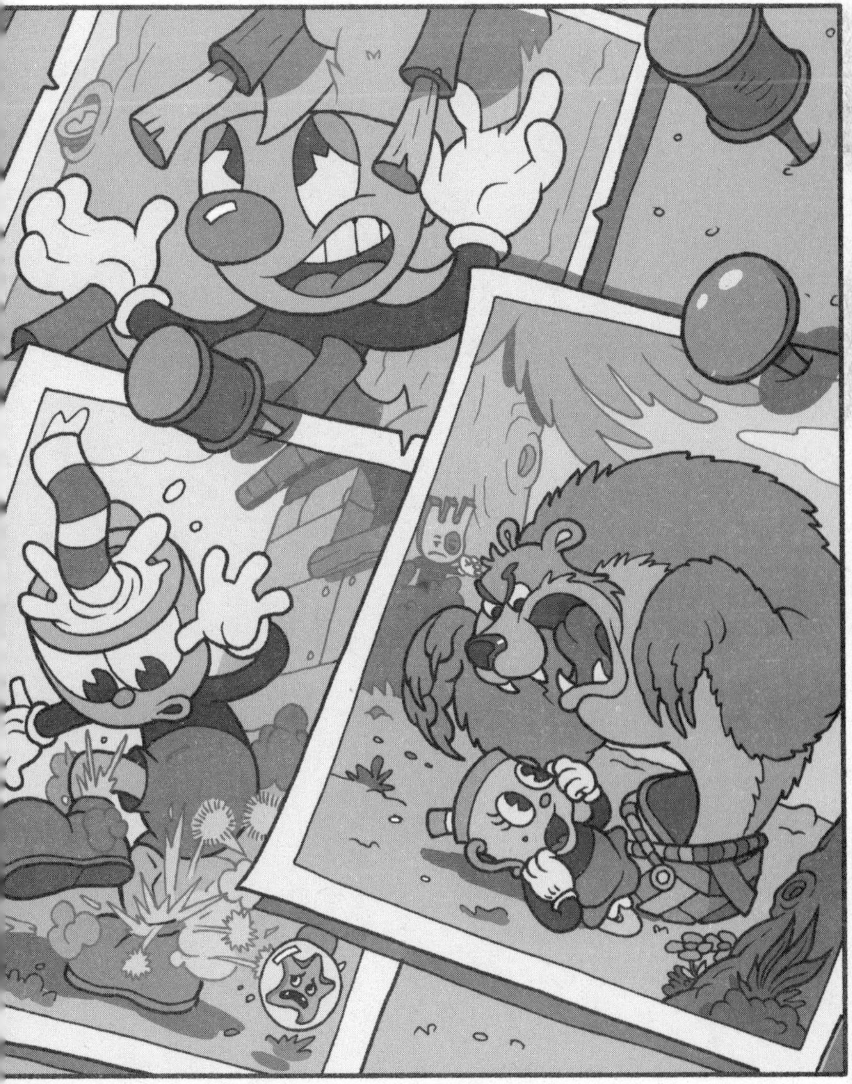

The weeks that followed would go down in Hootenholler history as the "Great Prank War." It was camp against camp, soldier against soldier, as they battled in a quest to bring their adversaries to their knees.

Wrongway was frantic.

"This has gone far enough!" he told the group. "You're ruining both camps and wasting your summer. Please stop this now!"

But it was too late. The wheels of destruction were already in motion, and there was nothing they could do but see it through to the end. The spiteful antics became daily affairs, and no one could keep track of where one prank ended and the next one began.

There was the time when Cuphead and a small contingent of Hootenhollers sneaked into the Punchafink camp during a birthday celebration. They watched as Baroness Von Bon Bon lit the candles on an enormous cake, which in turn ignited a long fuse that ran the length of the mess hall. Now, the interesting thing about this fuse is that it connected to a row of firecrackers that had somehow ended up in the shoes of every single Punchafink. One by one, they exploded, causing the campers to leap to their feet, knock over tables, tear down decorations, and ultimately send the massive party pastry flying into the air.

It was known as the "Hootenholler Hotfoot," and it was a rousing success.

Then, a short time later, there was the incident where the Punchafinks managed to replace Mugman's axe with one made out of rubber. Unfortunately, Mugman failed to notice this when he went out to do his wood chopping, and—*BOINNNNNNNNNNNG!*

The axe bounced between the log and Mugman's head over and over again until he'd been driven into the ground like a stake.

This was known as the "Chopper Flopper," and it, too, was a triumph.

As the days rolled on, so did the high jinks, until there were too many to count. No one could possibly remember them all, but a few did stand out as especially noteworthy.

The time Ms. Chalice opened her picnic basket expecting to find a peanut butter sandwich, but instead she found a live grizzly bear.

The time the Punchafink rooster blew his bugle for a morning inspection, but instead of playing a tune, he sent a spray of thumbtacks into the assembled campers.

The day the Punchafinks placed a stink bomb inside the shuttlecock during a particularly well-attended Hootenholler badminton tournament.

The time the Hootenhollers lined a trail with quick-drying cement just before the Punchafinks took their nature hike.

It was after that last prank that Cuphead, Mugman, and Ms. Chalice were making their way back to camp and having a wonderful time recalling the looks on the Punchafinks' faces as they marched along wearing huge concrete blocks where their boots should have been.

"That'll learn 'em," Ms. Chalice said. "Now maybe they'll think twice before they mess with Camp Hootenholler again!"

Of course, the only problem with that statement was that they'd said it after every single prank. And so far, there was no evidence the Punchafinks had thought even once, much less twice, before striking back with some outlandish scheme of their own. And so the feud went on and on and on.

Still, a good prank is a good prank, and the three of them were in high spirits.

"The best part is with those cement shoes, they can't chase us!" Cuphead said. "But let's take the long way back, just to be safe."

It was a sensible precaution. After all, they never knew when they might run into some Punchafink booby trap, or even one of their own that they'd forgotten about. So the trio bypassed the usual routes and made the long, meandering walk back over the mountain to avoid any possibility of a problem.

As they gained altitude, Mugman turned around and eyed the distant speck that was Camp Punchafink.

"Remember how nice that place was the first time we saw it?" he reminisced.

"Boy, do I, but we took care of that. Now it's a real dump!" Cuphead said proudly, failing to mention that, in fact, the feud had turned both camps into dumps. "And to think they were so worried about the 'curse of the mountain.' Jeepers, what a bunch of clods! What they shoulda been worried about is the curse of the Hootenhollers!"

Now, since this was their first time heading back to camp over the mountain, it took a while for the trio to get their bearings, and they marched until late into the night. Still, there was a moon out, and they all laughed and joked and sang little tunes as they made their way up the hill. But just as they were about to reach the top—

"Hey, don't be starin' at the moon! Watch your step, you hulkin' goon!!"

Needless to say, Cuphead was very surprised. The voice seemed to come out of nowhere. He looked to his left, then he looked to his right, and finally, he lifted his foot.

There, shaking his fist in a most unfriendly manner, was the smallest person Cuphead had ever seen.

"Gnomes!" said Ms. Chalice.

14

GNOMES IN THE GNIGHT

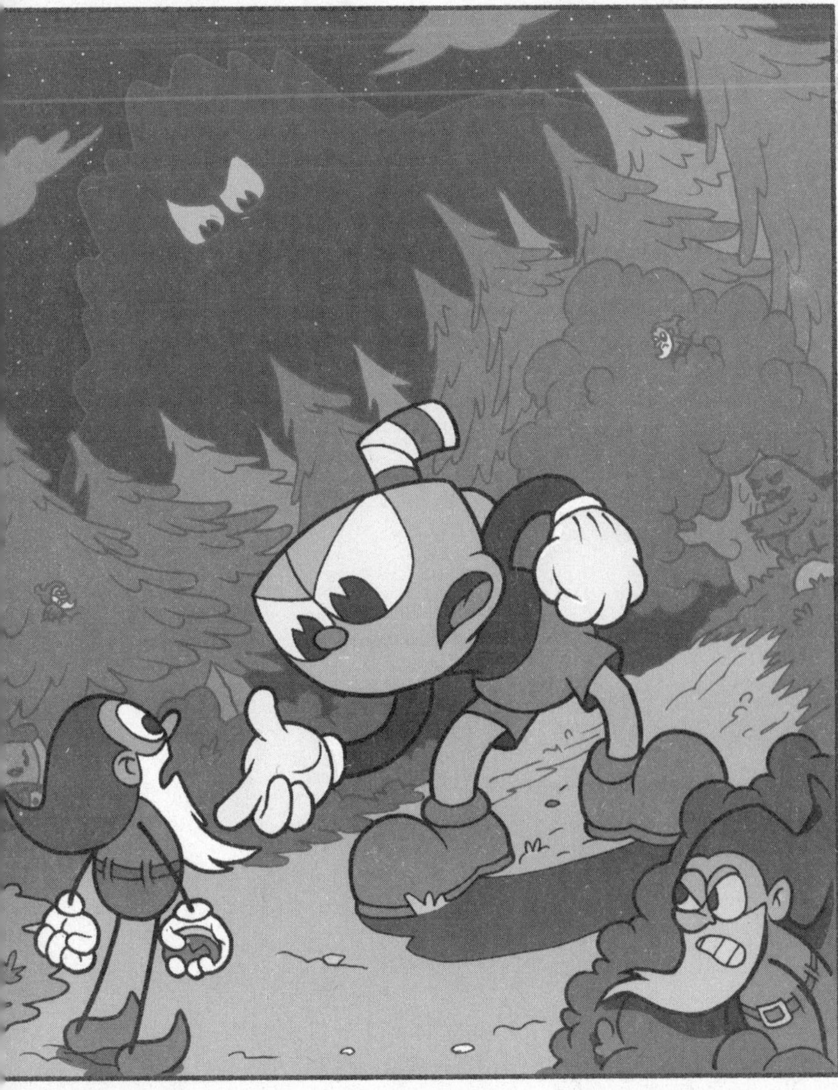

Cuphead carefully moved his foot away from the tiny figure, and he was just as cautious in choosing where to set it down again. After all, everyone knew that stepping on a gnome was very bad luck—well, at least it was for the gnome.

"I'm awfully sorry," said Cuphead. "I'm afraid I didn't see you."

"Oh, you didn't see me? What a surprise! Maybe you should check your eyes?" snapped the gnome, and he shook his fist and brushed the dust out of his long white beard. "Traipsin' through, laughin' and rompin', not carin' at all 'bout who you've been stompin'!"

Cuphead felt badly about what had happened, but he really didn't think it was his fault.

"Well, it is dark out here," he said. "And you *are* awfully small."

Oh dear. If you know anything about gnomes, you

know that this was the wrong thing to say. Gnomes are touchy about their size, and they don't appreciate having total strangers drop by to remind them they're among the forest's tinier folk. Naturally, the gnome was furious, and he scowled and grumbled and muttered the most insulting things about big-footed buffoons and large lumbering lummoxes. Then, for good measure, he took off his long, pointy hat and hurled it dramatically to the ground.

"Small, am I? Well, so says you! I could tell you a thing or two!" he shouted. "What makes you so sure I'm small? Could it be that you're too tall? A monster, a giant, an oversize lout—a behemoth who makes whole villages shout? If I were in your hulkin' shoes, I'd be careful 'bout the words I use!"

Cuphead had never thought about it that way. To a gnome, he must seem absolutely enormous. And while the little fellow made a very good point, Cuphead was not happy about the way he made it. After all, you can't call someone a big-footed buffoon and then expect to have them agree with you. The truth of the matter was that, from Cuphead's perspective, the gnome was miniscule and therefore had a responsibility to make those of normal size aware of his presence.

It was just common sense.

"Leapin' lizards, we can't constantly be walkin' around staring at our feet because we're afraid we might crush someone," he said, and he looked at the massive hillside surrounding them. "And how do you expect me to spot one little gnome in a place as huge as this?"

"One little gnome?" said the gnome.

And in the blink of an eye, everything changed. Suddenly, gnomes were popping up all around them. They were in the grass and the flowers and the trees and just about anywhere else you'd care to look. Cuphead never realized how many gnomes were out there in the unseen cracks and crevasses—why, for all he knew, Elder Kettle's house could be full of them! They were fascinating little fellows, and he bent over for a closer look. They all had long white beards and pointy red hats, but perhaps their most distinguishing feature was that none of them looked very happy.

Not the ones glaring up at Cuphead, anyway.

"Did you hear that? It's all our fault! Why should he be forced to halt?" the angry gnome told his kin. "This gargantuan goon can step where he pleases, and the blame is on you if it's your head he squeezes!"

Well, on hearing this, the other gnomes raised a terrible fuss, and they tugged on their beards and wiggled their noses and called Cuphead gnomish names he'd never even heard before. He tried to explain but couldn't get a word in edgewise. Finally, Ms. Chalice, who had been around much longer and was more familiar with the creatures of the forest, came to his defense.

"That's not what he meant, at all," she assured them. "Golly, if we'd known there was a whole village here, we would've been a lot more careful! But it wasn't intentional, we just made a little mista—"

Uh-oh. She wanted to take back the word the minute it left her mouth, but it was too late.

"Oh, a *little* mistake, was it?" said the very unpleasant imp. "You think you're so big, but you're smaller than some! Why, I know one who could squish you right under their thumb!"

Cuphead had heard quite enough, thank you very much. He didn't care for threats, especially those that involved being squished under giant imaginary thumbs. Not that he was worried, of course. After having a good look around, he was fairly sure no one here was capable of punching him in the kneecap, much less doing anything of the squishing variety. Still, that was no excuse for bad manners. So he politely asked the gnomes to clear the path and also to watch out for humongous feet, which couldn't always help where they landed. The gnomes were outraged! They resumed their name-calling and did so very loudly (because gnomes are only quiet when they want to be), and before long exasperated voices were echoing all across the landscape.

And that's when one of the gnomes, who appeared to be older and wiser than the others, waved his hat and got everyone's attention.

"*Shhhhhhhhhh!*" he said. "Will you be quiet? You don't want to start a riot! If you keep yellin' with that yap, you're bound to wake him from his nap!"

"Wake who?" asked Mugman.

But the gnomes didn't answer. Instead they scattered like leaves on a windy day. They hid themselves in bushes and in tree trunks and in the tall grass. As for the three travelers, they were very confused—and then they heard something.

It was a yawn.

15

A MOUNTAIN OF TROUBLE

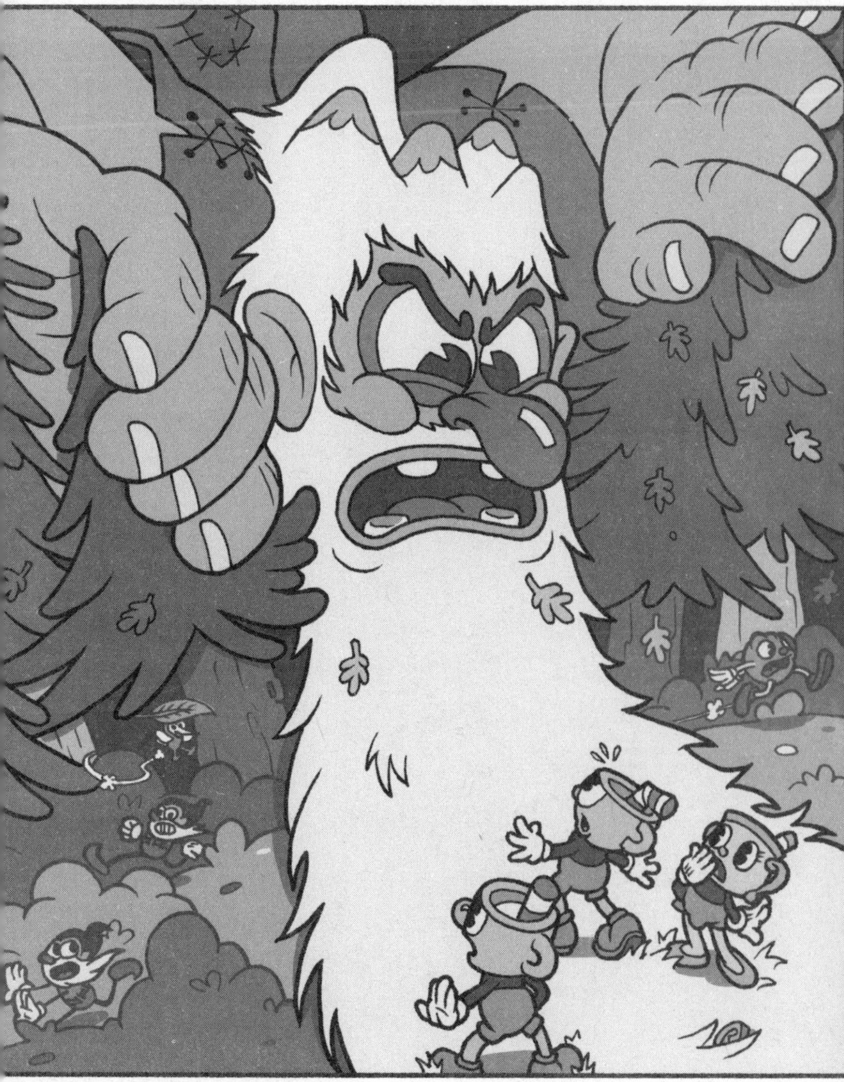

Of course, there are all different kinds of yawns. There's the secret yawn, which is the one where you turn sideways and try to pull it off without anyone noticing. There's the barrier yawn, which is where you cover your mouth with your hand to keep your uvula from escaping (as they sometimes do). And there's the bored yawn, which isn't so much a yawn as a way of telling someone they're not very interesting.

This was none of those.

It was, quite simply, the biggest yawn in the whole wide world.

YAWWWWWWWWWWWWWWWWWN!

The ground shook beneath the trio's feet, and they watched in horror as a huge, gaping mouth opened a short distance away. Had they not grabbed hold of a hackberry bush, they might very well have been pulled into it, and goodness knows where they would've ended up then. Fortunately, the vast opening soon closed, and the ground stopped shaking, and everything was calm again.

And yet Cuphead had the oddest feeling he was being watched—possibly because he was face-to-face with an enormous eyeball.

"Odsbodikins, who woke me from my slumber?!" asked a voice as big as all outdoors.

The gnome—the one who'd been very rude since the moment they arrived—crawled out of the tall grass and faced the giant eye.

"It was them, these three, this trio of raiders," he said. "They're trespassing, big-mouthed, destructive invaders!"

"No, we're not!" said Mugman. "We're campers!"

"Campers!" the voice roared. "I might have known. Why must I always be troubled with campers?"

Whoever this was clearly had a problem with campers. They sounded very annoyed, and Cuphead stepped in front of his brother.

"The truth is, we're just three friendly travelers who happened to be passing through," he said. "I'm Cuphead, this is Mugman, and that's Ms. Chalice. And who might I be speaking to?"

A gasp rose up from all the tiny hiding places.

"Oh, gracious sakes, it can't be true—you don't know who you're talking to?" the gnome said, sounding completely astonished. "Get down on your knees, stop being defiant! You're in the presence of Glumstone the Giant!"

Glumstone the Giant! Cuphead remembered the name from Cagney's campfire story, but he never for a moment thought such a creature could be real! If you recall, Cagney had said Glumstone was a huge and powerful mountain and someone you wouldn't want to cross, and now that the three friends had actually met him, they understood why!

The sun was just beginning to rise, and the mountain shook his head and stretched. Rocks rolled downhill like an avalanche, and the visitors grabbed the hackberry bush and held on tight. A moment later, with the glow of the sun breaking through the darkness, they got their first look at Glumstone in all his glory. He had a gigantic face, a shock of white hair, and a long, flowing beard that meandered down like a stream. He was as imposing a figure as they could imagine.

"I'm very sorry we disturbed you," Cuphead said. "We didn't know we were intruding."

The mountain reached out, grabbed him by the back of his shirt collar, and lifted him into the air. He took a long, careful look at the little cup.

"Kind of tiny to be a camper, aren't you?" he said. "I remember them being larger."

"They come in all shapes, and they come in all sizes," the gnome explained, "but they're all terribly rude and full of surprises! Why, this bunch was trudging right through our homes, crushing our crops, and stomping us gnomes!"

Glumstone frowned.

"Were you stomping my gnomes?!" he roared.

"No!" said Cuphead. "That is, I didn't mean to. We were just on our way back to camp."

The mountain raised an eyebrow.

"And what camp would that be?" he asked.

Cuphead gulped.

"Hootenholler," he said nervously.

Glumstone set Cuphead down beside his friends. Then he stroked his beard and rubbed his chin.

"Hootenholler, eh? That name sounds familiar. *Hmmmm*... I remember something about it from a long time ago. Now, what was that?"

"You cursed it," said Mugman.

Whoops. The answer just slipped out. Mugman hadn't done it on purpose. He just couldn't help being helpful.

Cuphead and Ms. Chalice gave him a very uncomfortable stare.

"Oh yeah," said Glumstone. "I forgot all about that! I used to be very big on curses, you know. Of course, that was the style back then. We used to have a curse for every occasion. Now, what was the one I put on your camp?"

The three friends buttoned their lips and shrugged. That is, until the mountain leaned in close and gave them a memory-jogging growl.

"Oh, now I remember!" Cuphead said as sweat poured over his brim. "The way we heard it, you said there were too many camps, and you were going to destroy one of them."

"And then you rained boulders down on Hootenholler," said Ms. Chalice.

The mountain laughed.

"Rained boulders? Where do they get these stories from?" he said. "I never did anything of the sort. I threw maybe one boulder—a tiny one. And, anyway, I was provoked."

"Provoked?" asked Cuphead.

"Sure," Glumstone said. "You see, there was this one camper who was making my life miserable. Every single day he'd start with the yodeling! Yodel, yodel, yodel, morning till night. And not good yodeling, mind you, it was awful! Oh, the agony! Now, let me see, what was his name? It was something like Yoo Hoo or Dodo or..."

"Yo-Yo," the three said together.

"Yeah, that's it!" said the mountain. "Say, how'd you know that?"

"Uh, lucky guess." Cuphead gulped.

The enormous peak squinted suspiciously but then continued.

"Well, anyway, I had to make it stop, and there's nothing like a boulder for getting someone's attention. Hey, that reminds me—I never did finish that curse, and there are still too many camps around here! So, I guess I might as well destroy... what did you say the name of your camp was again?"

"Hooten—" started Mugman, but Ms. Chalice quickly slapped a hand over his mouth.

"Now, just one minute!" she shouted at their humongous host. "The curse said you would destroy the worst of the two camps and leave the other one alone. Well, how do you know our camp isn't the good one? You wouldn't want to go back on your word, would you?"

Glumstone considered it.

"Eh, they're both pretty terrible," he said at last, and picked up a boulder. "That one over there ought to do."

He was looking in the direction of Hootenholler.

The three friends' eyes grew as big as tennis balls, and it was no wonder, because they realized they had made a dreadful mistake. They had to think of something quickly.

"Hey, I've got an idea!" said Cuphead. "What about a contest? It'll be Hootenholler versus Punchafink, and the camp that loses will be the one that has to go!"

Glumstone the Giant stroked his beard.

"Well, I guess that *could* be interesting," he said.

"And we'll devise the contests and monitor the races," said the gnomes. "And disqualify the first buffoon who steps upon our faces!"

They were looking straight at Cuphead.

"Yes, a competition—that should keep things lively around here!" the mountain said. "But I still get to smash something when it's over, right?"

"Oh, absolutely," said Cuphead.

"Then a contest, it is! We'll have it this Saturday," Glumstone declared. "And may the best camp win. . . . Or the worst. It doesn't really matter. As long as one of them ends up being a big pile of rubble, then it's all right with me."

16

MAY THE BEST CAMP (NOT) WIN

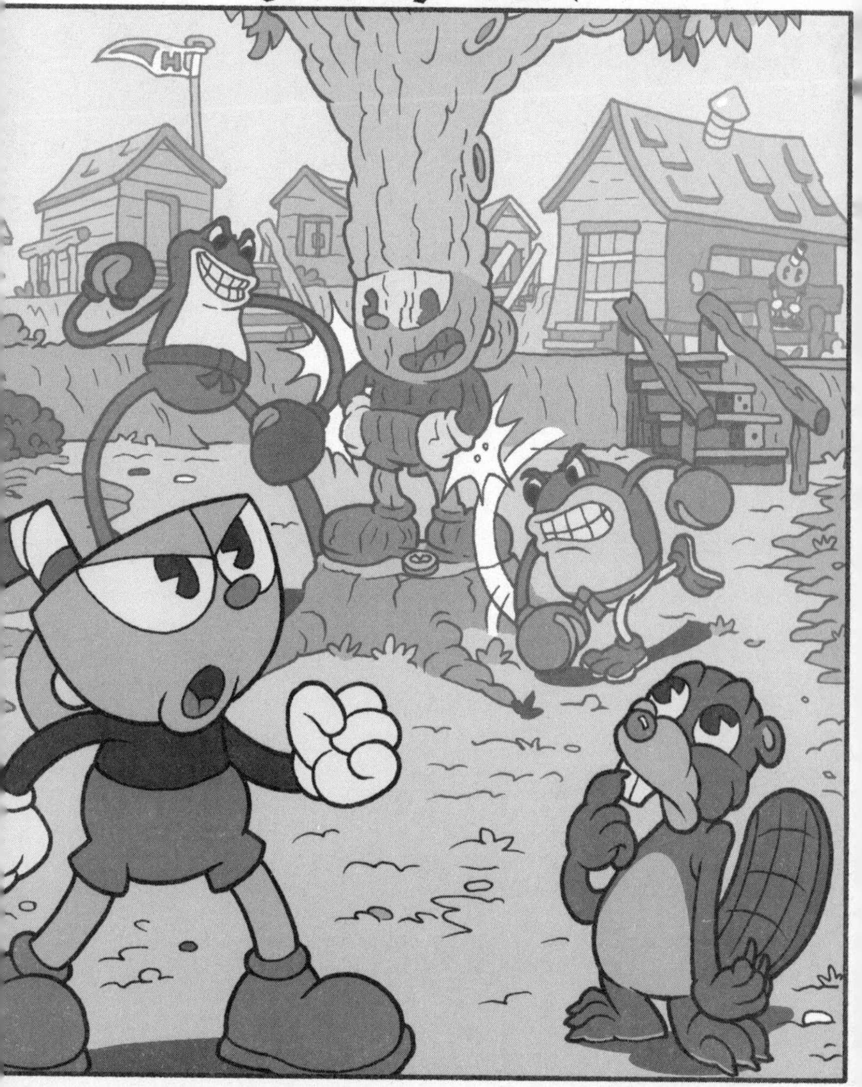

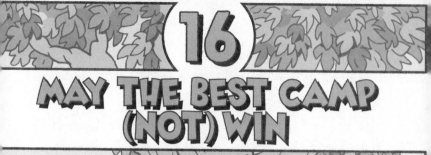

As they headed back to camp, the trio was filled with a tremendous excitement. Not only had they met Glumstone the Giant and lived to tell the tale, but they'd found a way to end the feud once and for all. And it was so simple! All they had to do was win a silly little competition. What could be easier?

Those horrible Punchafinks were as good as gone!

"We should have thought of this a long time ago," said Mugman.

Cuphead couldn't have agreed more. Oh, he enjoyed a good prank as much as the next fellow, but the situation had gotten out of hand. This feud had taken over their summer and turned both camps into absolute wrecks. And worst of all, no one was having fun anymore. But the contest would change that—the contest would change everything!

He could hardly wait to tell their camp mates.

After a long trek, the three friends arrived back at Hootenholler and marched triumphantly into the camp yard. They summoned everyone to join them.

"We have big news!" said Cuphead, and he stood up on a tree stump, because an announcement this important deserved a stage. "The feud with the Punchafinks is over!"

Well, needless to say, there was much rejoicing in the land of Hootenholler. The campers danced and leaped and cheered. They pulled the boards off the windows of their cabins to let in the long-banished sunlight. They tore down signs that said VICTORY FOR HOOTENHOLLER! and IF YOU SEE A 'FINK, RAISE A STINK! and A PRANK A DAY MAKES THOSE PUNCHAFINKS PAY! and joyfully shredded them into confetti.

"It's over! It's over! It's over!" they cheered.

Cuphead suddenly felt very uncomfortable. He'd expected the group to be excited, but not *this* excited. Perhaps he hadn't been clear.

"Now, when I said the feud was over, I meant *practically* over," he said, correcting himself. "But it will be soon. It's almost a sure thing."

The cheering stopped. In fact, there was no sound

at all. The crowd that had been so happy and excited only a moment earlier seemed very different now. Their ecstatic smiles had been replaced by blank stares of confusion.

"So is it over, or isn't it?" asked Canteen Hughes.

Cuphead looked out at the campers. He pulled at his collar.

"Well, it's like this," he said, and he told them the whole story about nearly stepping on the gnomes and meeting Glumstone the Giant and, finally, about suggesting they have a contest to decide which camp would remain and which would be destroyed.

"So you see, all we gotta do is win the competition, and the Punchafinks will be gone forever!" he said excitedly.

Of course, because he was Cuphead, it had never even occurred to him that there could be any outcome but complete and total victory. Ms. Chalice and Mugman felt exactly the same way, and why wouldn't they? The three of them shared a positive attitude and a can-do spirit that had gotten them through the toughest of adventures. And while defeat was always a possibility, they saw no reason to waste valuable brain space thinking about it.

But now, gazing at the stunned faces of the other campers, Cuphead began to wonder whether the competition had been a good idea. It meant risking everything in a contest against the Punchafinks, who were a formidable bunch to say the least. All of a sudden, he felt a new and very unpleasant sensation right in the middle of his stomach. Was this doubt?

"The thing is, if we win—"

Cuphead stopped. There was that word—*if*. Only a short time ago, he'd been so sure about the whole thing! Was it possible that he, Ms. Chalice, and Mugman weren't conquering heroes who were saving Camp Hootenholler? Might they actually be the instruments of its destruction?

The thought was terrifying. He sat down on the stump and rested his chin in his hands. Then a shadow appeared on the ground. When Cuphead looked up, he saw Ms. Chalice standing over him.

"Don't worry, Cuphead," she said, a knowing grin strung across her cheeks. "We just need to pump up some enthusiasm."

And with that, she walked to a nearby pump and began working the handle. But instead of water, out came—well, something else.

"Hello!"
"Hellooooo!"
"Helloooooooo!"
"HELLOOOOOOOOOO!"

It was the four Mels. They popped out of the spigot and burst into a rousing motivational number that went something like this:

TOUCH *your* TOES *and lift your* CHIN!
BOM *bom* BOM *bom*—
PUSH *your* LIM-*it and pull up a* GRIN—
BOM *bom* BOM *bom*—
SHOW *some* SPIR-*it, do a* VIC-TOR-Y *dance*—
BOM *bom* BOM *bom*—
THAT'S *the* WAY *to have a* SPORTING
   CHANCE!
HIT *the* ROAD! RAISE *the* BAR!
EX-ER-CISE *and it will* TAKE *you far!*
KEEP *on* RUN-*ning till you* WEAR *out your*
   SHOES
AND *by and by, you'll* FIND *that you're not* FIT TO
   LOSE!
OHHHHHHHHHHH—

PRESS *your* LUCK*!* CHASE *your* DREAM*!*
BOM *bom* BOM *bom—*
THINGS *are* NEV-*er quite as* BAD *as they* SEEM*!*
BOM *bom* BOM *bom—*
You'll NEV-*er see the* FINISH *line until you* BE-*gin!*
So PULL *this team to-*GETH-*er and get* FIT TO
     WIN*!*

As the words rolled out in the most tuneful way, the campers started to feel much better about things. After all, winning was just a matter of having the correct attitude. Why, with proper motivation and a little luck, anything was possible. So right there on the spot, the group started exercising using anything that was handy. They lifted logs and rolled rocks and leaped over hedges and climbed to the tops of very tall trees. They did push-ups and pull-ups and sit-ups (there's nothing like a good up when you're feeling down) and every other kind of calisthenic, and all to the inspiring sound of barbershop.

The Mels had done their magic, and the campers could barely contain their enthusiasm. Caught up in the excitement of it all, a pack of young beavers surrounded an elm tree and went to work. When they were through, the sturdy trunk had been transformed into a life-size carving of the hero of the moment—Cuphead!

•　•　•　•　•

That night, as the campers roasted their marshmallows over an open fire, they talked excitedly about the upcoming contest.

"We'll make those Punchafinks wish they were never born!" said Mugman, and he put a marshmallow on each end of a stick and used it as a dumbbell.

"Sure! You just wait until Saturday," Ms. Chalice said. "We'll fix their wagon, and how!"

"Oh, really?" said a voice from the darkness.

A moment later, a girl in a pirate hat emerged from the woods. She was followed by a tough-looking delegation of Punchafinks, some of whom Cuphead had already met.

"What do you want, Cora?" he said.

The pirate girl smiled.

"Oh, nothing," she told him. "We just thought we'd take one last look at Hootenholler before it's turned into a pile of rubble."

Cuphead's eyes narrowed, and he put on his fiercest scowl.

"You'll have plenty of time for sightseeing after Punchafink gets pulverized," he said. "So why don't you step on an egg and beat it?"

"Why don't you make us?" said Cora.

"Oh yeah?"

"Yeah!"

"Oh yeah?"

"YEAH!"

The campers watched as these two masters of the snappy comeback continued their verbal joust (no camp rivalry was complete without a vigorous round of taunting). Finally, Cora had heard enough.

"Look, this is your final warning," she said. "Stay away. If you show up Saturday, bad things are going to happen."

"Yeah? Like what?" demanded Cuphead.

The entire Punchafink delegation broke out in sinister grins. Then Ribby and Croaks stepped out of the pack and made their way to the large, wooden likeness of Cuphead.

"Hit it, boys," said Cora.

And that is precisely what they did.

The frogs' boxing gloves were little more than a blur as they punched and pounded the statue without mercy. When they'd finished and the dust had settled, the Hootenhollers saw what remained of the former elm tree.

It still looked like Cuphead—only now the figure had a black eye, an arm in a sling, a leg in a cast, and a very, very sad expression on its face.

The real Cuphead gulped. Still, he wasn't about to let these intruders have the last laugh.

"Big deal," he said. "Two can play that game."

And without a moment's hesitation, he grabbed the marshmallow off the end of his stick and quickly molded it into a soft, fluffy replica of Cora. Then, as a symbol of his defiance, he popped it into his mouth.

"Aigggggggggggggh!" he screamed, which was understandable, since a marshmallow fresh from the flames is approximately the same temperature as molten lava.

Quickly, he dashed to a nearby rain barrel and stuck his head inside.

The Punchafinks howled.

"Enjoy your camp," Cora said between giggles. "Because after Saturday, it'll be nothing but a memory!"

17

WINNERS & BRUISERS

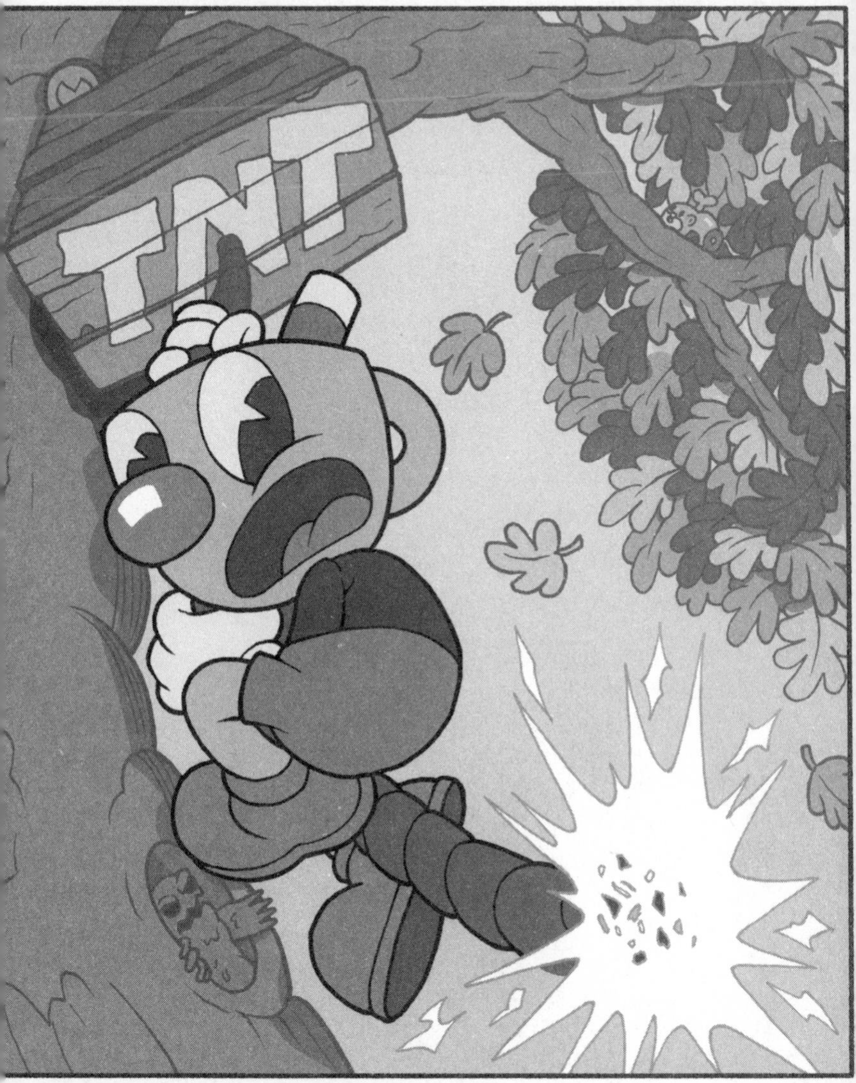
TNT

Saturday began with the camp rooster strutting out to his perch, opening his clucker, and proclaiming:

"SO LONG, HOOTENHOLLER! IT WAS FUN WHILE IT LASTED!"

Needless to say, this was not the vote of confidence the campers were hoping for on the day of the big match against the Punchafinks. Still, a wake-up call was a wake-up call, and they dutifully filed out of their cabins and assembled in the camp yard.

"Good morning, champions!" said Wrongway, using his most reassuring tone. "Now, I know you've all been training very hard—"

"Like that'll make a difference," muttered Cagney.

"—and that you've been eagerly awaiting this day. All I can ask is that you do your very best and remember that Hootenholler is proud of you. Okay, follow me!"

Inspired by the director's words, the Hootenhollers

snapped to attention and, in a noble, straight row, marched off to meet their destiny. Unfortunately, destiny was actually in the opposite direction, but Wrongway simply whirled round on his heels and led the team back down the trail.

At last, they reached their destination, and the campers saw the terrible mountain. Glumstone the Giant was staring at an enormous pocket watch and looking severely annoyed.

"There you are!" he bellowed. "I was beginning to think you weren't going to show."

"Sorry," said Wrongway. "We were, um, delayed."

Glumstone frowned and put away his watch.

"Oh well," he said. "Let's get on with it."

And with that brief and grumpy opening remark, the contest to decide which camp would stay and which would be wiped from the face of the earth had begun.

• • • • •

The groups gathered together in a large circle while one of the gnomes read a lengthy list of rules.

"No bitin', no fightin', no kickin', no trickin', no talkin' back or we'll give you a lickin', no pullin' noses, no rubber hoses, no steppin' on gnomes AND NOT ON OUR ROSES! No callin' one another hard-hearted names, no complainin' about the games, no givin' up just to save you a beatin', and most important of all, none of your cheatin'!" he said.

Then he rolled up the scroll, stuck it inside his beard, and led everyone over to the first event, the rope climb.

* * * * *

"Jeepers, are you sure you want to do this?" Cuphead asked.

"Absolutely," said Mugman.

"And you won't be scared?"

"Well, maybe a little," Mugman told him. "But look, there's a bell."

Sure enough, hanging from a high branch in a very tall tree was a shimmering silver bell—and the contestant who got there first would get to ring it!

"It's not every day a fella gets the chance to ring a bell, you know," Mugman said.

Cuphead nodded. Of course, he could've pointed out that there were bells on their front door, the telephone, Elder Kettle's typewriter, the alarm clock, and both their bicycles, and that Mugman could ring them anytime he wanted. But it would've been a shame to spoil his excitement.

"You get up there and ring it once for me," he said instead, and went to join the others in the cheering section.

Mugman grabbed hold of the thick, dangling cord and gave it a practice tug. He didn't know very much about ropes, but this one certainly seemed sturdy. He wondered how hard it was to climb one of these things. Oh well, he'd find out soon enough.

In the meantime, since he didn't want to appear rude and had nothing better to do, he turned to greet his opponent—which, as it happened, was Croaks.

"It's a long way up there, isn't it?" Mugman asked cheerfully.

"A long way down, too," said the frog.

Mugman didn't know why, but there was something about the look on Croaks's face that gave him the willies. Oh well. There was no time to worry about that now—the race was starting.

"Climb up and give the bell a ring, and then you'll win the whole darn thing," said the gnome with the scroll in his beard. "We'll be watching from below. Now on your mark, get set, and go!"

Well, right out of the gate, Croaks made a tremendous leap (you know how frogs are about

212

leaping) and was a quarter of the way up the rope before Mugman even left the ground.

"Mugman!" yelled Cuphead. "You're behind!"

Mugman looked down. "What about my behind?"

"Just go!"

And go he did. As it turned out, Mugman was a natural-born climber. In no time at all, he was neck and neck with the ascending frog, and a few seconds later, he had passed him completely. Now, considering what was at stake, you'd think the sight of Mugman blazing by would've made Croaks nervous. But the thing is, he didn't seem nervous—not one little bit. In fact, he was smiling.

But Mugman paid him no mind. He just kept climbing and climbing and climbing, because now there was nothing between him and that shiny silver bell except clear blue sky. Well, that and a large rectangular-shaped object with a burning fuse sticking out of it.

Hmmmmm, he thought, studying the thing.

It looked very much like a big, harmless box.

"Cuphead," he called out. "What does *T-N-T* spell?"

Cuphead, who was always up for a spelling quiz, considered the matter.

"Oh, that's easy," he shouted back. "*T-N-T* spells— oh no!"

Of course, he did not really mean to say *oh no!* What he meant to say was that TNT isn't a word, at all; it's a set of initials that stand for *Terribly Noisy Thing*. But before he could explain—

BOOM!

Poor Mugman. His face looked like a freshly toasted marshmallow. There were little puffs of smoke rising out of his straw, and his rope had completely disintegrated. As he lingered there in midair, he had the most awful feeling this was not going to be his day. Eventually, he looked down and—seeing nothing underneath him—dropped like a fifty-pound hailstone.

Fortunately, the ground broke his fall.

"Mugman! Mugman! Speak to me!" said Cuphead, shaking his brother by the shoulders.

Slowly, Mugman opened his eyes. He felt very well, all things considered, though he did wonder why little bells were circling his head like a merry-go-round.

"Do you hear ringing?" he asked.

The truth is, Cuphead did hear ringing, but not

because of a nicked-up noggin. It was for a much more painful reason.

Croaks had reached the top of the rope. The Punchafinks had won.

• • • • •

No one knew how the Terribly Noisy Thing had gotten there, though the gnomes strongly suspected it was defective rope. At any rate, there was nothing anyone could do about it. Little problems were to be expected in a contest like this, and the important thing was to keep moving forward. So after awarding the Punchafinks their points, they quickly herded everyone over to the next event, the tug-o'-war.

"We'll win this one, for sure," said Cuphead. "After all, if there's one thing Hootenhollers are good at, it's pulling together."

More determined than ever, he and Ms. Chalice joined a crew of their camp mates at one end of a very long rope. Directly across from them, a row of smirking Punchafinks (smirking being the official camp facial expression) were holding the other end. But the most interesting part of the event was what lay in between the two groups—a very deep, very messy mud puddle.

"You can do it, Hootenhollers!" Mugman called from the cheering section. "But keep your eye on that rope—they're trickier than you'd think."

Just then, a tiny referee appeared and climbed up on a tree stump.

"Tug and pull with all your might," he said, "or else you'll need a bath tonight."

This was good advice, and the Hootenholler team prepared themselves for a long and strenuous battle. Anxiously, they waited for the sound of the gnome's whistle, and when it arrived—they pulled!

Oh, and what a pull! This was no casual, easygoing, Saturday-afternoon-on-the-hillside sort of pulling; it was an intense collective tug, the kind that moved boulders and freight trains and elephants.

But it did not move the Punchafinks. Not one inch.

"Pull harder!" cried Cuphead, and the crew dug in, yanking and tugging until their arms felt like severely overcooked noodles.

And still the Punchafinks did not budge. Worse, they seemed completely unaware anyone was trying to move them. Cora, who was at the head of her group, yawned lazily, let go of the line, and stretched as if she were just waking up from a nap. Then, having grown bored with this game, she nodded to her team, took hold of the rope again, and gave it a nice, gentle tug.

WHOAAAAAAAAAAA!

The Hootenhollers moved forward. In fact, they glided forward, and very quickly, too, because they found it impossible to stop. The reason was simple—the earth beneath Cuphead's team was coated in a thin layer of extra-slippery axle grease. So, one by one, the helpless Hootenhollers slid to the edge, toppled over, and plunged face-first into the deep, dark mud.

Covered from head to toe in gooey sludge, they emerged from the pit to the sound of mocking laughter.

"Oh well, being a Hootenholler's a dirty job, but somebody's got to do it," Cora screamed. "The good news is—not for very much longer!"

Then the entire Punchafink troop burst into hyena-like howling, which, for Cuphead, was almost unbearable.

"*Psssst*, Cuphead," whispered a muddy Ms. Chalice. "I hate to sound like a sore loser, but somethin' tells me this bunch is up to no good."

Cuphead was thinking the exact same thing. Not only had the Hootenhollers been standing in grease, but he had a sneaking suspicion Cora and her team were nailed to the ground! Still, he didn't want to be accused of mudslinging—at least not while he was wearing so much of it.

"It doesn't matter, anyway, we'll still beat them," he said confidently. "Trust me, the next event is in the bag!"

• • • • •

Cuphead pulled Cuppet out of the bag.

Well, it wasn't so much a bag as a small brown suitcase with silver hinges and a black handle, but the important thing was that it was the perfect size for carrying a puppet.

"It's time for the talent show, Cuppet," said Cuphead. "You're not nervous, are you?"

"No, I'm not nervous," said Cuppet. "I'm high-strung!"

This was the kind of joke you could only get away with if you happened to be hanging from a cluster of strings, which, of course, he was. You see, Cuppet was a puppet, and an extraordinary one, at that. He looked like a miniature Cuphead with the same striped straw, the same red shoes, and, most essentially, the same love of applause. Together, they couldn't lose!

All right, they could lose, but Cuphead was very hopeful they wouldn't. He had already seen the Punchafinks' musical act ("See You Later, Mr. Tater" performed by the Sal Spudder Trio) and thought it could be topped. But they'd have to put on their best show to do it.

The pair practiced their stage smiling as they waited to be introduced.

"And now," said the gnome announcer, "put your hands together, get off your tuffet—it's those hearty Hootenholler hoofers, Cuphead and Cuppet!"

Naturally, this brought wild applause from the Hootenholler section, while the Punchafinks in the audience were as quiet as a bashful mouse in the library.

Cuphead and Cuppet moved onto the stage.

Tappity-tappity-tappity-tappity-tappity-tappity-tap.

Now, you're probably wondering why they were making odd, rhythmic *tap-tap-tap*ping noises, which any judge was bound to find distracting. Well, the truth is, it was all part of the act. You see, tap dancing numbers were extremely popular at the time, and if you threw in a few jokes along the way to keep things lively, that was icing on the cake.

"So, Cuppet," Cuphead said in a loud, clear voice, "was that you I heard laughing a minute ago?"

"Yes, it was, Cuphead," said Cuppet. "I was laughing at Glumstone."

A gasp rose up from the audience, and for a very good reason. Few things were riskier than laughing at a giant, especially one as mean and grumpy as Glumstone. Suddenly, an enormous shadow fell on the stage, and the crowd heard a menacing rumble.

Meanwhile, the show went on.

"Laughing at Glumstone?" said Cuphead. "Isn't that dangerous?"

Tappity-tappity-tappity-tappity-tappity-tappity-tap.

"Not at all," replied Cuppet. "He's HILL-arious!"

For a long, agonizing moment, no one made a sound. And then they heard something.

"Ho-ho. . . . Ho-ho-ho. . . . HO-HO-HO-HO-HO-HO!"

Glumstone was laughing.

"HILL-arious!" he shouted gleefully. "Because I'm a hill! Oh yes, that's funny! A mountain joke! Ha-ha-ha-ha-ha!"

After hearing Glumstone's reaction, the Hootenhollers joined in and laughed right along with him. Cuppet had taken a dangerous situation and turned it into a punch line, which, of course, is the mark of a great entertainer.

The only problem was that the mountain was chuckling so vigorously that he nearly shook them off the stage. Fortunately, he managed to calm himself, and the performance—*tap-tap-tappity-tap*—continued.

"Oh, Cuphead," said Cuppet. "Can you loan me a dollar?"

"But, Cuppet, what happened to the dollar I gave you yesterday?" hammed Cuphead.

"I gave it to a gnome," said the puppet.

"What did you do that for?"

"I had to," Cuppet told him, then paused for just a beat. "He was a little short!"

"BWA-HA-HA-HA-HA-HA!" roared Glumstone. "It's true—gnomes *are* short!"

And then he hooted and howled and shook the ground all over again. And this time, even the Punchafinks laughed! (The gnomes, on the other hand, didn't even crack a smile, but that's because gnomes have no sense of humor.)

Cuphead was delighted. Things were going very well, and now it was time for their big finish—a paddle-and-roll-spin-kick-turn step that was always a real crowd-pleaser. They shuffled out to the edge of the stage and started the routine, but something seemed off. You see, while Cuphead was doing a *tap-tap-tappity-tap*, Cuppet was doing a *tap . . . THUD . . . tap . . . THUD* and falling down a lot.

"Cuppet," Cuphead said. "You're missing a leg!"

"AAGGGGGGHHHH!" screamed Cuppet.

Cuphead had no idea what could've happened to it. But then, out of the corner of his eye, he spotted the wooden leg moving across the stage all by itself. Or so it appeared. It wasn't until he took a closer look that he found the limb was actually being carried away by an army of tiny bugs. They were headed toward an official-looking black travel bag with writing on the side:

ACME TERMITES

"WE CHEW TILL THE JOB IS THROUGH!"

WOOD REMOVAL—REASONABLE RATES

This was outrageous! One of the first rules of show business was that you did not take a tap dancer's leg in the middle of a performance. It just wasn't done! But what upset Cuphead most of all wasn't the termites—it was who they were working with. You see, holding the black travel bag was none other than Sal Spudder.

Now there was no doubt—the Punchafinks were cheating!

Cuphead quickly grabbed the limb away from the inconsiderate insects and returned it to his partner.

"I'm sorry termites tried to eat your leg, Cuppet," he said.

Cuppet just smiled.

"That's all right," he said. "It might not have been our best performance—but at least it was tasteful!"

Good ol' Cuppet—he always knew how to go out on a joke.

18

HOOTENHOLLER GETS A LEG UP

This was turning into a disaster. After a few more disappointing events, the score was Camp Punchafink—fifty, Camp Hootenholler—zero.

"Come on, come on, let's get on with it," Glumstone said impatiently. "It's getting late and I've still got to crush Camp Hootenholl—I mean, the losing camp—when this is over."

He really didn't need to correct himself. The outcome was beginning to look inevitable, even to the Hootenhollers.

"How are we going to make up fifty points?" asked Mugman.

"One event at a time," said Cuphead, who was more determined than ever now that he knew for certain the Punchafinks were cheating. "Now go out there and win this one!"

The "one" Cuphead was referring to was the javelin

throw. It involved tossing a spear-like pole as far as possible into a field, with the longest effort being declared the winner.

"You can do it, Mugman," Ms. Chalice said encouragingly.

Mugman smiled, but he'd never felt less confident. After all, he'd lost the rope-climbing event, and this one didn't even have the opportunity to ring a bell. And if that weren't bad enough, he was going up against Cora.

Cora was a pirate, and everyone knew pirates were experts at handling pointy things. Why, they used swords and harpoons the way other people used toothpicks. He didn't stand a chance.

"When you're ready, take your throw," yelled an especially long-bearded gnome standing in the field. "Let's see how far these sticks can go!"

Cora warmed up her throwing arm.

"Good luck," Mugman told her.

"Save it," she sneered. "You're gonna need all the luck you can get."

Then she picked up a javelin, approached the line, and proceeded to make a terrifying toss. The spear traveled so fast and so far that it sent tiny figures throughout the meadow screaming and running for cover.

"That thing's as sharp as twenty knives! Look out, gnomes—run for your lives!"

Finally, it came down at the farthest end of the field, landing so close to the judging gnome that it pinned his beard to the ground.

"That throw was strong and mighty far—a new camp record, that one are!" he called out.

Mugman hung his head. He could never compete with that throw and really didn't see the point of trying. But Elder Kettle hadn't raised him to quit.

He looked at Wrongway, who had stopped by to watch the contest.

"Any advice?" he asked.

Wrongway thought for a moment.

"Well," he said, as if delivering an expert analysis, "the important thing in a javelin contest is to use the wind currents. That's the key to a good throw. And judging from the current conditions, I'd say you should throw—"

He held a single finger in the air.

"That way," he said.

Unfortunately, he was pointing in the opposite direction from the javelin field.

"But, Wrongway," said Mugman. "That's—"

"Now, my boy, you mustn't argue with science," the director told him. "Remember, if there's one thing we compasses know about, it's direction."

Mugman sighed. What choice did he have? So he shrugged, turned his back to the javelin field, and let the long, slender pole fly. And for a beginner, he didn't think he did badly, at all. The javelin gained considerable height and distance, and except for the fact that it was traveling in completely the wrong direction, it was a perfectly respectable toss. He couldn't wait to see where it landed.

But as it turned out, he did wait. He waited and waited and waited, and still the javelin did not land. It couldn't land, and for a very good reason—while the projectile was still in the air, it was snatched by a passing eagle, who carried it far off into the distance.

"Ha-ha-ha-ha-ha! Ha-ha-ha-ha-ha!" laughed Cora.

The other Punchafinks laughed, too, and even Mugman had to smile. Imagine having his toss intercepted by a large bird! He supposed that was something that only happened occasionally even to experienced throwers.

Still, the fact remained that the javelin was gone, the Punchafinks had won, and that was all there was to it.

Well, almost all...

You see, while the eagle did carry Mugman's spear a very long way, she did not carry it forever. She dropped it down into the last place anyone would've expected—Old Forceful's spout.

Old Forceful, of course, was the geyser who had angrily expelled the campers' bus while they were on their way to Hootenholler. Well, as it turned out, he found javelins to be even more annoying than buses, so with an enormous *pa-TOOOOOO!* he spewed the thing back into the air.

And what a spew it was! The javelin flew so high that several clouds had to move out of the way to keep from being shish kebabbed. It sailed past the javelin field and all the way onto the archery field, where it scored a perfect bull's-eye.

Now, it goes without saying that this was the kind of thing that didn't happen every day, which is why the judges talked it over for a good, long time. And after scratching their heads and twisting their beards, they made an announcement.

"A throw like that does not make sense," said the head gnome. "So Mugman has won both events!"

Yes, as hard as it was to believe, with a single throw, Mugman had won not only the javelin competition but the archery contest, as well. The Hootenhollers were on the board!

• • • • •

As much as the team would've loved to stand around celebrating, there was no time. The three-legged race was starting and they wanted to be there to cheer on Ms. Chalice and Tully as they paired up against Ribby and Croaks.

"Call me bonkers," said Ms. Chalice, "but I've got a bad feelin' those frogs are up to somethin'."

"The wise person does not dwell in the shadow of suspicion, but lights the way with their own goodness," said Tully.

Ms. Chalice raised an eyebrow.

"So you're telling me you trust those two?"

"Not as far as I could throw them," said Tully, and he showed her just a hint of a smile.

The rules of the contest were simple. Each team would consist of two racers with one of each of their legs cinched together, and the first team across the finish line would be the winner.

"What has three legs and wins a race?" said the gnome official. "The team that has the quickest pace!"

Then he blew a small silver whistle, and the race was on! Ms. Chalice took off like a lightning bolt—unfortunately, she was a lightning bolt that was dragging a turtle, which was a significant problem. You see, while Tully was a very dedicated and sincere racer, his tortoise physique was not built for speed.

"You're doin' swell, Tully, keep it up!" Ms. Chalice urged him.

"I'm—*puff, pant*—trying," said Tully.

Ms. Chalice gave him a reassuring grin. It was true Tully wasn't the swiftest runner in the world, but he was doing his very best. And the good news was that the race was still surprisingly close. With Cuphead, Mugman, and their camp mates shouting encouragement and rooting them onward, the pair had managed to match the frogs stride for stride. But just when it was starting to look like they had a real chance of winning—

SPROINGGGGGGGG!

They tripped. Or to be more precise, they *were* tripped. This was a devastating setback, but the worst part was that it was not their fault. You see, the rope that had been used to tie Ms. Chalice's leg to Tully's had also been tied to an oak tree. And they knew very well who was behind it! Ms. Chalice was exasperated.

Tully put a hand on her shoulder. "I know you're disappointed," he told her. "But remember, every setback is a lesson in disguise."

Suddenly Ms. Chalice's eyes brightened.

"A lesson, of course!" she said excitedly. "Tully, it's high-time we taught them how this game is played!"

Quickly, she untied the rope and—without so much as a how-do-you-do—climbed into Tully's shell. It was a very tight squeeze, but by poking her legs through the bottom holes, she was able to lift her partner completely off the ground. And now that those turtle legs weren't slowing them down, the team was uncommonly fast. With Ms. Chalice running like a sprinter, they promptly covered the entire course and pulled up alongside the fleeing frogs.

"What's the matter, fellas?" she said "Haven't you ever seen a two-headed turtle before?"

And then the speedy shell-mates leaned forward and broke the tape at the finish line.

Well, as you can imagine, the Punchafinks were furious! Ribby and Croaks raised the most awful fuss, until finally the gnome in charge agreed to investigate.

"The rules say four legs there cannot be," the gnome explained. "And when I count these, I see one, two, and—"

Tully, who at the moment was dangling both legs in the air, quickly pulled one of them back inside his shell.

"Three," said the gnome.

And being that they had the right number of legs, and there was nothing in the rules against two racers sharing a shell, the tiny judge declared Ms. Chalice and Tully the winners.

This, combined with the excellent news that their campmates had won the thumb-wrestling, limbo, and balloon-animal contests, meant Team Hootenholler was on the verge of an amazing comeback.

As for whether it would continue, that was all up to Cuphead.

19

DOUBLE-CROSS-COUNTRY RACERS

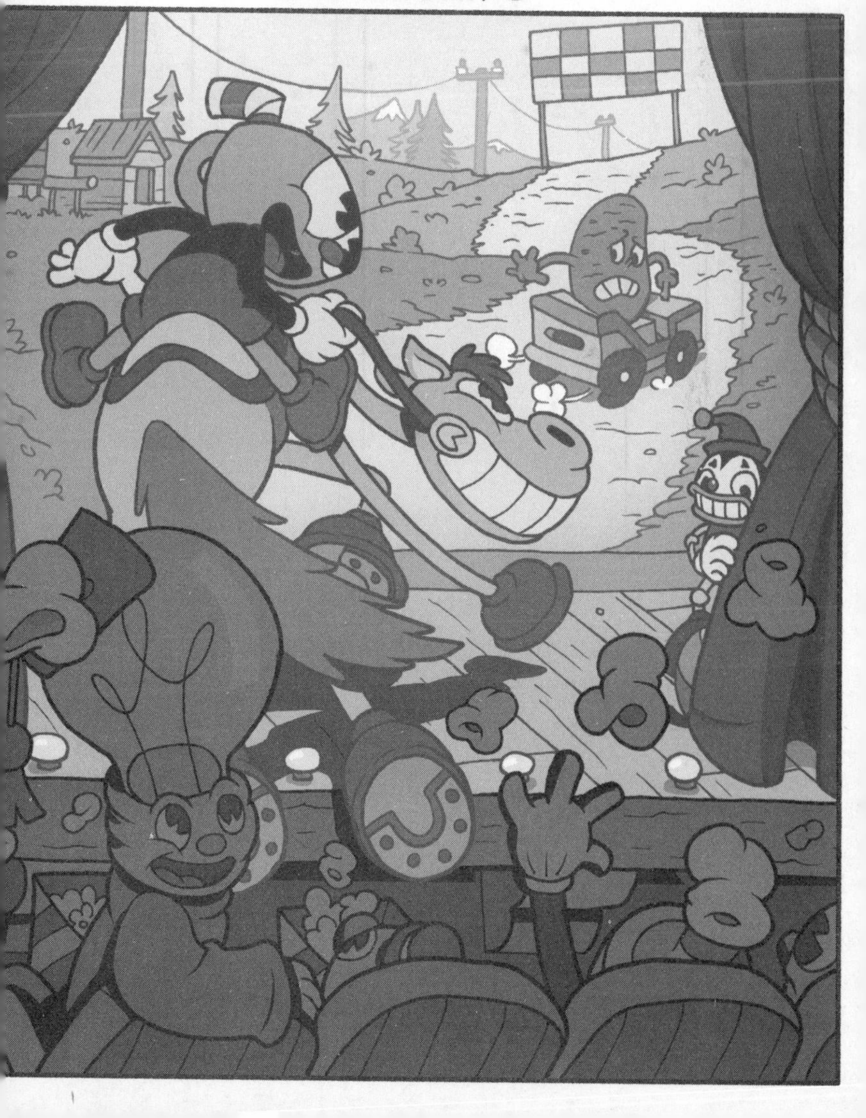

Everyone agreed Cuphead was the obvious choice to represent Hootenholler in the cross-country event. After all, if someone was going to run the most brutal, exhausting, and torturous race of their life, it might as well be the camper who got them here.

Cuphead wasn't worried. He'd been running long distances for years (just because he was being chased by a wild beast or an angry neighbor didn't mean it wasn't useful experience) and felt well-prepared for the challenge. And with his positive attitude and extra-special good luck charm—he never raced without it—how could he possibly fail? Of course, winning wouldn't be easy. Any contest designed by gnomes was bound to have tricky obstacles and treacherous terrain.

And speaking of tricky and treacherous...

"Well, well, well, if it ain't ol' Twinkle-toes," Sal Spudder grunted.

Cuphead's eyes narrowed. Out of the entire Punchafink team, wouldn't you know he'd be going up that against that smug, smirking potato! It was just the motivation he needed.

"I hope you're hungry, Sal," he said. "Because you're about to eat a big, heapin' helpin' of my dust."

The two glared at each other. This was no longer about curses or camps. It was something deeper, more personal. They were gladiators entering the arena, and when this day was over, only one of them would be left standing.

Well, unless they were both standing, which was always a possibility. You couldn't stop someone from standing just because they lost a race. Still, the loser would definitely be slouching under the terrible weight of defeat, and nobody liked a sloucher.

"Gee, Cuphead," said Ms. Chalice. "Do you think you can take this palooka? He's awful big."

Cuphead waved away her concerns.

"Eh, nuthin' to it," he said. "You know what they say: The bigger they are—"

"The easier it is for them to squash you under their thumb," said Mugman.

The three of them looked straight up. Glumstone was hovering menacingly above the group.

"I'm tired of waiting!" bellowed the mountain. "Let's get started. The rules are—aw, heck, there are no rules. Cross the finish line first and you win, got it? Now on your mark, get set, et cetera."

Needless to say, the crowd was stupefied. An impatient mountain was nothing to be ignored. Cuphead rubbed his chin.

"Now, when you say 'et cetera,'" he said, "do you mean—"

"I mean GO!" yelled Glumstone.

Well, the racers didn't waste another second. They streaked away from the starting line and set a blazing pace as they tore down the opening stretch. No sooner would one take the lead than the other would come roaring past him. It was a relentless, back-and-forth, seesawing battle, and neither was willing to give an inch. They were still running shoulder to shoulder as they crossed over the first hill, and Cuphead wondered how long this could go on.

Suddenly, Sal turned to him.

"I've got to hand it to you, Twinkle-toes, you're some

kind of runner!" said the potato, and then he smiled and gave him a friendly pat on the back.

Cuphead could hardly believe it. Was this the same untrustworthy tater who had tried to steal Cuppet's leg during the talent contest? It certainly seemed out of character. Then again, it was hard to tell about these things—perhaps the heat of competition had brought out Sal's sporting side. Whatever the reason, Cuphead was genuinely moved.

Only not in the direction he wanted to be.

"WHOAAAAAAAAAA!"

Poor Cuphead. For reasons he could not explain, he was being pulled backward at an alarming speed, and then—

CLANNNNNNNG!

He found himself attached to a large and powerful magnet. It was sticking out of a clump of bushes along with four rubbery green arms.

"Look who decided to come see us," said Ribby.

"Well, ain't that nice? Must be our magnetic personalities!" added Croaks, and the two howled in the fiendishly funny way cheaters do.

Cuphead frowned. How had he let himself be fooled again? And by such an obvious ruse! Sal hadn't been giving him a pat on the back—he'd been hanging an iron horseshoe off the back of Cuphead's shirt! And now here he was stuck to a magnet having to listen to these ridiculous frogs. Well, they wouldn't get away with it! The judges were going to hear about this shameless act of cheat—

Then he remembered. It wasn't cheating—there was no cheating, because Glumstone had said there were no rules. Which meant the Punchafinks could pull any funny business they wanted, and there wasn't a single thing he could do about it.

"I don't have time for this!" he yelled, wriggling his shirt free. The frogs made a quick lunge at him, but Cuphead grabbed their wrists and shoved their hands through the curved space in the horseshoe.

"Hey, we're stuck. Get us out of here!" cried Croaks.

"Sorry fellas," Cuphead said with a wave. "But I've got a race to win!"

And he took off down the trail after Sal.

Now, by this time, the potato had a substantial lead, but Cuphead remained as positive as ever. The magnet had been a setback, but with Ribby and Croaks out of the way, he felt sure his troubles were behind him. Of course, that was before he saw what was ahead of him.

It was Drop-Dead Gorge!

Yes, Drop-Dead Gorge: the deepest, widest, most dangerous trench on the Inkwell Isles. The only way across it was a rickety old bridge that anyone would think twice about using—three times if they were the cautious sort. Cuphead, however, did not think even once. He simply rushed out onto it, and then, quite unexpectedly, stopped.

You see, waiting on the other side was Sal—and he was holding a large pair of scissors.

"You wouldn't!" said Cuphead.

"Oh, but I *would*," said Sal.

And then—*SNIP!*—he did.

He cut the ropes, and the long, wooden bridge began tumbling into the gorge below. One by one, the planks fell away, and Cuphead bounced from board to board as he rushed back to solid ground.

Sal let out a long, irritating laugh.

"What a shame—looks like the bridge is out," he yelled. "Ain't that too bad?!"

And then he turned around and strolled slowly down the path.

And why wouldn't he? There was no reason to hurry now—the race was over. Anyone who tried to cross Drop-Dead Gorge without a bridge was in for a very long fall, and the stop at the end would be no picnic, either. So, Sal whistled a little tune and took his time, enjoying what was turning out to be a lovely day.

There was only one problem: His opponent was Cuphead. And Cuphead never gave up. Why, the thought didn't even cross his mind. Instead, he pulled a bow tie out of his pocket, strapped it around his neck, and spun it like a propeller. Then he stuck out his arms and climbed skyward like an airplane.

Soon he was soaring across the gorge without a care in the world, and then—

RAT-A-TAT-TAT-TAT-TAT!

He was under attack! Looking down, he saw Sal firing up at him with a peashooter. Cuphead dipped his wings and made a steep dive. Then, pulling out his own shooter, he returned fire, sending Sal running for cover. Peas were flying in both directions as Cuphead lined up for an aerial assault, but just as he was starting his approach—

WHAAAAAAP!

He took a direct hit in the bow tie.

Smoke streamed from the tie, and it spun slower and slower until, finally, it sputtered to a halt.

Cuphead was going down! In desperation, he headed for a clearing in the trees. Bravely nosing himself onto the ground, he skidded across the soil, and came to a bumpy but very welcome stop.

"Whew!" he said, spitting out a mouthful of dirt and a very annoyed earthworm.

"Wormeater!" cried the worm.

Meanwhile, Sal continued to trudge along in a leisurely way, confident he had stopped his opponent once and for all. Why, the nerve of that little pest— didn't he know the race was over before it started? Well, he knew it now! The thought of the crashing cup put a smile on his face—but it was not there for long. Because when he turned around, he saw Cuphead coming down the path in a cloud of dust.

"So, he thinks he can outsmart me, does he?" Sal muttered. "Well, I'll fix him!"

And that's when he tried his dirtiest trick yet. On the side of a very large boulder, he painted a picture of a tunnel (Sal was a gifted artist who'd been drawing since he was a tot), and next to it, he put up a sign. It said, SHORTCUT.

"That ought to do it," he said. "When Twinkle-toes

hits this wall, they'll have to scrape him off with a spatula."

Then he chuckled to himself and hid in the bushes to watch the fun.

A short time later, Cuphead came roaring round the bend. Without a moment's hesitation, he raced up to the painted picture of the tunnel—and ran right through it.

Sal was livid! There was nothing more upsetting than putting together a fiendishly evil scheme only to have your victim refuse to cooperate. This was unacceptable! And even worse, it was impossible! Storming out of his hiding place, he immediately began pushing and shoving against the boulder with all his might. It was solid—rock-solid—as any boulder should be, which only made him angrier. But if Cuphead could do it, so could he! The spiteful spud took a deep breath, backed up several feet...and stopped. You see, there was an odd noise in the air that hadn't been there earlier. It sounded like a whistle. Peeking inside the tunnel, Sal saw a tiny light that was getting bigger by the second.

"A train!" he shrieked, and quickly peeled the drawing off the side of the boulder and threw it on the ground. Then he let out a long, relieved sigh, took one step... and fell into the big painted hole.

Now, you might think that was the last anyone saw of Cuphead's opponent, but you're forgetting about the train. Almost instantly, it burst out of the hole heading straight upward with Sal hugging the front of the engine.

"YOWWWWWWWWWWW!" he cried, his voice growing softer and softer as he faded into the clouds.

As for Cuphead, he was still zipping down the path completely unaware of his rival's predicament. He didn't dare slow down, since for all he knew, Sal was still in front of him. But even Cuphead could only run at full speed for so long, and he stopped for just a moment to catch his breath.

And that's when—*VROOOOOOM!*—Sal came zooming past him. He was riding a tiny car.

(That's right, a car. If you thought a little thing like being hit by a flying train would stop Sal Spudder, you know very little about villainous potatoes.)

For Cuphead, this was the last straw.

"So that's how it's gonna be, eh? Well, two can play at that game," he said, and he put a pair of fingers in his mouth and gave a loud whistle.

And sure enough, in practically no time at all, a trusty horse came racing up the trail and stopped alongside him. (This was something he'd learned on his favorite radio program, *Wyatt Burp: Rootin' Tootin' Root Beer Mug*, which fortunately was the horse's favorite program, as well.)

More determined than ever, Cuphead promptly mounted up, and the two of them blazed after the motorized Sal. But just as they crossed over the hill, they saw a sign that said FREE MOVIE TODAY. HORSES WELCOME!

Well, if you've been paying any attention, at all, you know this was obviously another of Sal's tricks. Cuphead also had his suspicions. Still, free movies didn't come along every day, especially ones that welcomed horses, and the opportunity was simply too good to pass up. The galloping duo excitedly rushed into the theater.

Then, while they sat there in the dark sharing a bag of popcorn, a picture came on the screen. It was an action-packed flick, a picture about racing, and they watched as a driving potato streaked down the—

"Driving potato?" yelled Cuphead. "The race!"

In a flash, he and the horse mounted up and

sprinted right into the movie screen (this is an excellent shortcut if you ever find yourself needing to get somewhere in a hurry), and a moment later, they were pulling up alongside Sal.

As they moved down the path, the racers battled back and forth—horse against car, potato against cup—ramming and pushing each other while they headed toward the final stretch.

But Sal's bag of tricks wasn't empty yet. He took out a pencil and drew a circle on the horse's saddle, and next to it he wrote *Ejection Seat.* Then—*BOIIIIIIIIIIIING!*—he pushed the button.

Cuphead was launched up, up, up into the air and came down in a distant field. Naturally, Sal was very pleased with himself, and now that his opponent was far off course, he quickly ditched the car and trotted toward the big red stripe that said FINISH LINE.

He could sense victory—the line was only a hundred feet away! Then fifty feet! Then twenty! Then ten! And then, before anyone could do anything about it, it was behind him.

Yes, you heard that correctly—Sal Spudder crossed the line first.

The Punchafinks erupted in an exuberant round

of cheers. They danced and celebrated and mocked their rivals, who would soon be without a camp. It was all over—the Hootenholler team couldn't catch them now. Camp Punchafink had won the competition!

A minute later, Cuphead came running across the big red stripe, but it no longer mattered. He felt terrible about letting the team down. All the Hootenhollers looked devastated.

Well, all but one.

Ms. Chalice, you see, did not look devastated. In fact, her expression hadn't changed a bit since Sal crossed the line. She even hummed a cheerful little tune as she grabbed a broom and strolled over to the race course.

"Goodness gracious, will you look at all this dust?" she said. "I can't believe they let this place get so dirty."

And with that, she started to sweep over the big red stripe. It wasn't until the dust was completely swept away that everyone noticed something peculiar. Just below the writing that said FINISH LINE, there was another line that said 100 YARDS THATAWAY. A large red arrow pointed down the path.

"Well, will you look at that?" she said. "I guess this race isn't over, after all."

The Punchafinks stopped cheering. The Hootenhollers stopped feeling sorry for themselves. And as for Cuphead and Sal Spudder, they looked at each other, scowled, and broke out in a dead run. Now they were headed for the *real* finish line!

Only this time, Sal had no tricks left. All he could rely on was his foot speed, which, unfortunately for Cuphead, was considerable. Cuphead panted and puffed and did his very best, but it was no use. He could not pull ahead of the bigger, stronger potato.

"Admit it—I'm faster!" said Sal. "You can't keep up!"

"No, I don't think I can," Cuphead said sadly, and he reached into his pocket. "I guess I won't be needing this anymore."

And with a little sigh, he pulled out his good luck charm.

You do remember Cuphead's good luck charm, don't you? The extra-special one he always carried when racing? Well, as it turned out, the luckiest thing he ever did was throw it away. That's because this particular charm was not a rabbit's foot or a clover or a found penny—it was a lead bowling ball. And the instant he tossed it into the air, he experienced an amazing burst of speed. He easily flew past Sal, who seemed absolutely stunned—possibly because the very lucky charm came down on his head.

Feeling fresher than he had the entire race, Cuphead shifted into high gear and—*ZOOM!*—stormed across the finish line!

This time, the Hootenhollers were the ones cheering and singing! They were very happy because they had tied the score—fifty points apiece. That meant the winner of the last contest—the obstacle course relay—would be the camp to survive the curse of the mountain!

20

MUGMAN FACES DE-FEET

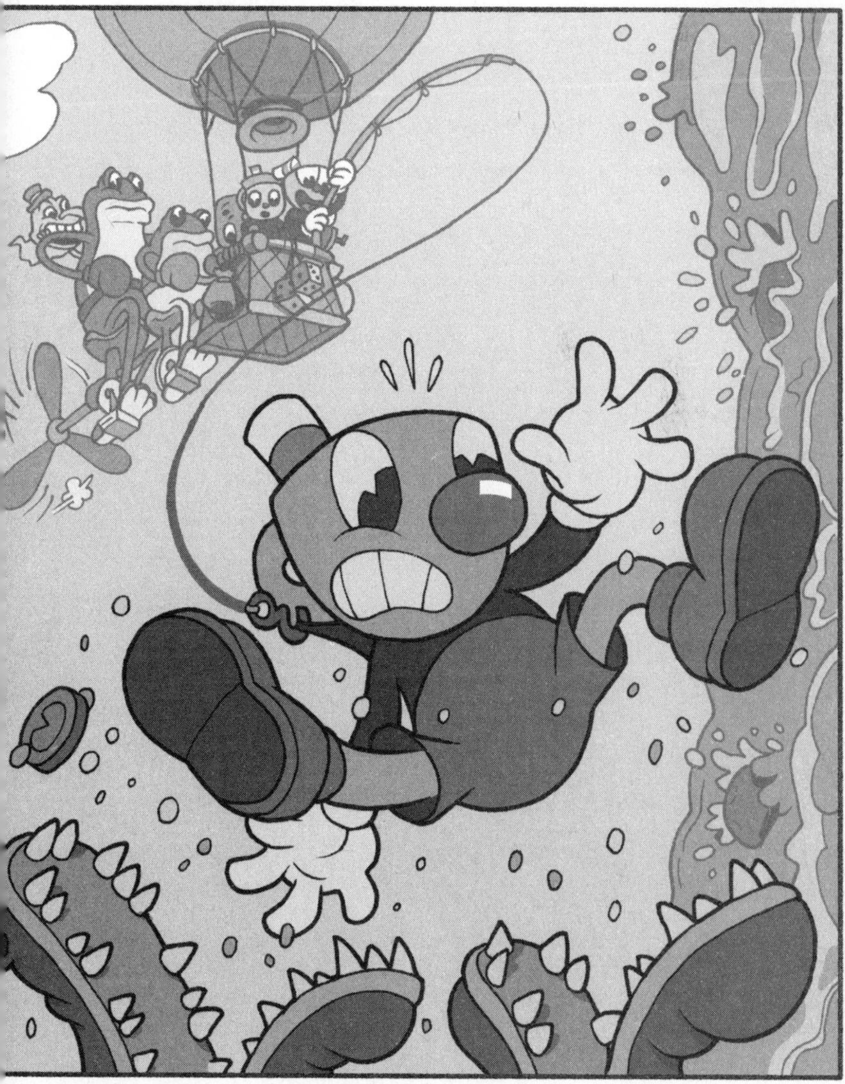

It had all come down to this. The obstacle course was the most rigorous sporting event ever devised by gnomes, and that was saying something. It consisted of seven excruciatingly difficult challenges: rolling a log across the river, dashing through a tire maze, crawling through a narrow tunnel, swinging on a flying trapeze, climbing over a high wall, bursting through a ring of fire, and, finally, whacking a carnival-style strength tester with a mallet to ring the bell of victory. Fortunately, since it was a relay race, no one camper would be forced to perform every task, and the Hootenhollers had selected a very reliable group of competitors to represent them. Oh, maybe not as reliable as the group representing the Punchafinks, but Cuphead had every confidence in his team. Still, if they were to have any chance at all, they'd need to get off to a strong start, and he was glad to see Mugman taking his position for the first leg.

"So . . . ready to roll?" Cuphead asked his brother.

Rolling, you understand, is a pretty big part of the log roll.

"To be honest, I'm a little nervous," said Mugman, trying to find his footing atop the thick, floating timber. "I thought the river would be more like Elder Kettle's kitchen."

But as it turned out, the two had almost nothing in common, which was disappointing. You see, Mugman's only previous experience doing anything close to the task at hand was the time he'd accidentally stepped on Elder Kettle's rolling pin and wobbled across the entire kitchen floor before crashing unceremoniously into the china cabinet. It wasn't much, but it was something.

"You'll be fine," Cuphead told him. "All you have to do is beat—"

He craned his neck to see who Mugman would be competing against. Then he gulped.

"Oh, criminy," he muttered.

It was Buzz Sawyer.

This was a problem. You see, Buzz Sawyer was absolutely enormous. How enormous? During a late-night raid, Cuphead had spotted him in the Punchafink camp and naturally assumed he was a grizzly bear. But Buzz was not a bear; he was 100 percent beaver, or perhaps even 200 percent based on his size. The only thing Cuphead knew for certain was that his presence here was very bad news for the Hootenhollers.

After all, there's no one in the world who knows more about logs than a beaver. They build with them, live in them, and sometimes have them for breakfast. Also, a beaver's webbed back feet are perfectly suited for rolling things across rivers, which was bound to come in handy.

"Don't worry about him. You'll be great out there," Cuphead said reassuringly.

"You don't think I'll embarrass myself?" asked Mugman.

But before Cuphead could say a word, they both heard a very beaverish snicker.

"Eh, there's nuthin' to it," bragged Buzz. "It's easy as fallin' off a log!"

And then he quickly spun the big brown trunk back and forth under his feet as if doing a kind of woodsy tap dance. It was sickeningly impressive.

Cuphead rolled his eyes and turned back to Mugman.

"Don't mind him. Just get across the river," he said. "I'll take it from there."

And with that, he went to assume his place at the relay's second obstacle, the tire maze.

Watching his brother walk away left Mugman with an odd, squishy feeling inside, but there was nothing he could do about it now. Because at that moment, a very tiny official with an even tinier whistle appeared at the starting line.

"On your mark, get set—try not to get wet," rhymed the gnome.

TWEEEEEET!

For something so small, the whistle made a surprising amount of noise, and Mugman's legs instinctively began pumping like two pistons in a revved-up engine. His log rolled slowly at first, then picked up speed, and before he knew it, he was neck and neck with the busy beaver. Needless to say, this did not sit well with Buzz. He hadn't expected this to be a competition, and he squinted his eyes and flapped his feet until they were nothing more than a blur.

But no matter how fast he rolled, the determined Hootenholler stayed right alongside him.

Now, the thing about log rolling is that it takes a lot of concentration. So it was no wonder that Mugman didn't notice the slender paintbrush cutting through the river like a shark's fin. It headed straight for him, and when it arrived, Ribby's slimy green hand emerged from the water and painted the beam with a thick coat of very sticky glue (which, of course, was cheating, and if that shocks you, then you haven't been paying attention and are far too trusting of frogs). Naturally, Mugman wasn't aware of any of this, and he only realized something was wrong when his feet came to an abrupt and very inconvenient stop.

"WHOAAAAAAA!"

Poor Mugman. Hopelessly stuck to the spinning log, he turned round and round and round like a noodle on an eggbeater. He was becoming quite dizzy and more than a little annoyed, but just when it looked like there was no escape from this dreadful predicament— *SHOOOOOOOOOOOOM!*—he slipped right out of his shoes and was hurled up, up, up into the air.

Well, as every lumberjack knows, a spinning

log packs a furious fling, and Mugman traveled a considerable distance before splashing down into the river. The point where he landed was nowhere near the obstacle course—though it was uncomfortably close to something else.

"Flatfoot Falls!" he gasped.

Flatfoot Falls was a very tall, very powerful waterfall that overlooked the foothills (which are exactly like regular hills, but shaped like feet) and was widely known to be one of the most dangerous locations on the Inkwell Isles. This wasn't merely because anyone going over the edge would be in for a terrible plunge—though that was unpleasant enough—it was because this was the preferred gathering place of a ferocious and constantly hungry congregation of alligator shoes. No creature in the foothills was quite as alarming, and if you'd ever seen their cold, unblinking eyelets and long, wagging tongues, you'd understand why!

These fearsome fiends of footwear were sneakier than sneakers, slipperier than slippers, and strong as an oxford. Luckily, they were at the bottom of the falls, and Mugman was at the very top.

If only he could've stayed there.

You see, as a river nears a waterfall, the current

becomes extremely strong, and though Mugman pushed and paddled with all his might, he could not break free. Before he knew it, he was at the very edge of the great spill, and a moment later—

"AHHHHHHHHHHHH!"

He was over it.

The little mug fell and fell and fell and fell. And then, quite suddenly, he stopped. That's because a drifting tree branch had become wedged between two rocks, and Mugman was wedged in the branch.

Now, if you've never tumbled over a powerful waterfall and found yourself stuck in the knothole of a large branch suspended above a gathering of ravenous alligator shoes, you should consider yourself lucky. As for Mugman, he was not enjoying it one bit, and for a very good reason.

He was worried about the race.

Yes, even as he faced grave peril, this was the fear that consumed him. After all, a loss in the relay meant that Camp Hootenholler would be shut down and destroyed, and for Mugman, that was a far worse fate than what awaited him below. He didn't know how he would ever face his friends again.

But he was about to find out.

"Holy smoke!" yelled Ms. Chalice, who was standing on the riverbank at the top of the falls. "What are you doin' down there?"

"Oh, just hangin' around," said Mugman.

"Don't worry, we're coming to get you!" Cuphead called out.

When Mugman looked up, he saw his brother's face peeking over the side—and many more faces, as well. It appeared that the entire camp had come to his rescue, and he was very touched.

"No hurry, take your time," he shouted.

It was typical of Mugman, who didn't like rushing people under any circumstance, and certainly not when they were doing him a favor. Still, he privately thought a little rushing wouldn't be the worst thing in the world, especially since the situation had recently become a bit more urgent.

You see, he was no longer alone on the branch. Two woodpeckers (which are the rudest of birds, as any tree will tell you) had landed on each side of him and begun pecking away like a pair of jackhammers.

"Excuse me," said Mugman politely. "Would you mind not doing that right now? This limb is the only thing keeping me in the air."

The woodpeckers stopped pecking.

"Did you hear that, Mr. Beaksley?" said one of the birds to the other. "He wants us to quit pecking this branch."

"I did hear that, Mr. Feathers," Mr. Beaksley replied. "Pure selfishness if you ask me. I mean, did we tell him not to get stuck in a waterfall?"

"Of course not. It's none of our business," said Mr. Feathers. "Our business is finding wood and then pecking it. Oh, look, here's some now! Well, back to work."

And the two of them resumed their enterprise as diligently as ever.

Meanwhile, the Hootenhollers had come up with a rescue plan.

"Mugman!" Cuphead yelled to his brother. "Grab the end of this stick!"

Then he lay on his stomach and extended a fairly long, exceedingly skinny twig over the side of the falls. Mugman held out his hand.

"I don't think I can," he shouted.

Actually, he could barely even see it.

"*Hmmmm*," said Ms. Chalice, studying the problem. "Maybe his arms are too short."

And, in fact, his arms were too short, but that was only part of the trouble. The major dilemma was that Flatfoot Falls was a very, very tall waterfall, and even the lengthiest stick in the forest wouldn't be nearly long enough to reach Mugman. It was a real head-scratcher, all right. But as the campers stood there pondering their next move, Cuphead heard a rustling in the trees.

A moment later, Wrongway, Cagney, Ollie, and Quint marched out of the woods.

"Never fear, help has arrived," proclaimed Wrongway. "And we brought a rope!"

A rope! Of course! Cuphead wondered why they hadn't thought of it sooner. A rope was just what they needed, and this was a fine one—thick and sturdy and very, very, very long.

"Now, everyone grab hold, and we'll run it over the side," said Wrongway.

One by one, the campers took hold of the rope and ran it over the falls. It easily reached Mugman, which was wonderful news, or would've been if it had stopped there. But it didn't. Instead, the rope extended all the way to the river below, where it caught the attention of a rather large and curious alligator shoe.

First he sniffed it. Then he pawed it. Then he slurped it down like a gigantic strand of spaghetti. In an instant, the rope rushed through the fingers of the rescuers and vanished into the one place no one would dare go after it.

"Oh dear," said Wrongway.

His concern was understandable. The camp's best rope had just been turned into an appetizer, and judging by the industrious bobbing of the woodpeckers, the main course would not be far behind.

The campers needed a miracle. What they got was—

"Punchafinks!" said Ms. Chalice.

Indeed, the entire population of Camp Punchafink was standing directly behind them. Cuphead didn't know how they'd managed to creep up so quietly, but he was in no mood for their antics.

"In case you haven't noticed, we're busy right now," he snapped at them. "So if you've come to gloat, take it somewhere else."

The Punchafinks moved toward their rivals.

"We didn't come to gloat," said Cora. "We came to help."

And right there on the spot, something extraordinary happened. Cora linked her arm into

Cuphead's. Then Ribby joined arms with Ms. Chalice. Baroness Von Bon Bon united with Wrongway, Croaks linked with Tully, Buzz and Ginger merged at the elbows, and so on, until next to every Hootenholler, there was a Punchafink, and next to every Punchafink, there was a Hootenholler. Sal Spudder, being the biggest and strongest of the group, latched himself to a tree, and then the campers fanned out to form a living ladder extending all the way to the rim of the waterfall.

Cuphead—very carefully—stepped over the edge.

"Take it easy. I've got you," Cora assured him.

"And I've got you," Ms. Chalice said to Cora.

What no one said out loud (but everyone was thinking) was that, in that instant, they all had one another, and the past troubles between them no longer mattered. For the first time in a long, long, long time, Hootenhollers and Punchafinks were on the same side.

Steadily, the living ladder moved lower and lower and lower.

"Jeepers, I'm almost there!" groaned Cuphead, and he turned to Cora. "Can you grab my ankle?"

Obligingly, Cora took hold of Cuphead's ankle and

suspended him upside down until he was just above the helpless Mugman. Cuphead stretched and reached, but try as he might, he couldn't manage another inch.

He would never give up, of course. It wasn't in his nature. Still, Mugman saw the look of defeat in his brother's eyes.

"Oh well, you did your best," he said, managing a grin. "Thanks for trying. It was good of you to drop by."

It was a gut-wrenching moment for everyone involved. Mr. Feathers, who had stopped pecking to watch the proceedings, shook his head.

"That's a real shame, that is," he said. "I thought they were going to make it."

"You and me both," said Mr. Beaksley. "It's too bad, really. You know how I love a happy ending."

And then the two of them sighed and went back to their pecking, because they had a schedule to keep, and there was no use lingering over a lost cause. It had been a valiant effort, but it was over, and everyone knew it.

Well, almost everyone.

"Step aside, comin' through! Seems we've got some work to do," said a little figure in a red hat.

It was the gnome Cuphead had nearly stepped on,

and he was leading a long procession of tiny rescuers down the line of interconnected arms.

"You?" said Cuphead, sounding surprised. "I mean, I appreciate that you want to help, but aren't you sort of—"

The gnome frowned and poked Cuphead in the nose.

"Unless you want your kin to fall," he grumbled, "the next word you say best not be *small*!"

Cuphead swallowed the lump in his throat and held out his arm like a bridge.

The gnomes crossed it. Then, from the tip of his finger, they linked themselves together end to end. But before they could reach their destination, the limb collapsed, and the helpless mug plunged toward a certain doom! Quickly, the last gnome snapped out a line from a fishing rod, hooking Mugman by the collar.

"You'll be all right, just wait and see," he said. "Now all you campers, pull on three!"

And on the count of three, every single Hootenholler and Punchafink and gnome pulled with all their might. And then—

WHOOOOOOOOOOSH!

Mugman was free as a bird. In fact, he even looked like a bird. That's because the enormous yank had sent him flying over the gnomes and the Hootenhollers and the Punchafinks and the falls and the trees and the river, and he did not come down again until he was back at the obstacle course.

There, his momentum carried him across the log roll, through the tire maze, and into the crawling tunnel, which ejected him like toothpaste from a tube. This launched him onto the trapeze, and he did a loop de loop that sent him over the climbing wall, through the ring of fire, and onto the strength tester, where he bounced off the platform, rocketed up the tower, and rang the bell with his head.

When Mugman at last found himself back on solid ground, he was battered, dizzy, and more than a little confused.

"Well, it's about time," roared Glumstone the Giant. "Looks like we finally have a winner!"

Yes, that's right—he said *winner*. You seem surprised.

Oh, did you think Camp Punchafink had already won the race? It's a perfectly understandable mistake. Cuphead and the others had made the same assumption. But the truth is, the Punchafinks had felt so badly about what had happened to Mugman that they didn't bother finishing the contest before going to investigate.

And now, without the slightest effort on his part, Mugman had single-handedly completed every obstacle and saved Camp Hootenholler.

The *camp*-etition was over.

Well, as you can imagine, when his camp mates arrived back at the mountain and learned what had occurred, they were ecstatic! They burst into cheers, lifted Mugman onto their shoulders, and paraded the camp banner around the hillside like a battle flag. Proudly leading the way was Cuphead, and he was smiling from ear to ear, because this was the happiest day in Hootenholler history!

There was absolutely nothing that could spoil this glorious moment for him—and then he saw the Punchafinks. They were not smiling or cheering, because they had no reason to celebrate. For them, the end of the race meant the end of their camp, and the agony of coming in second best showed in their faces.

All of a sudden, the Hootenhollers didn't feel like celebrating anymore. Their victory had lost its sweetness. Slowly, they wandered across the field and stood beside their former enemies.

Cuphead put his hand on Cora's shoulder.

"This isn't right," he said.

21

A BLOW TO THE RIVALRY

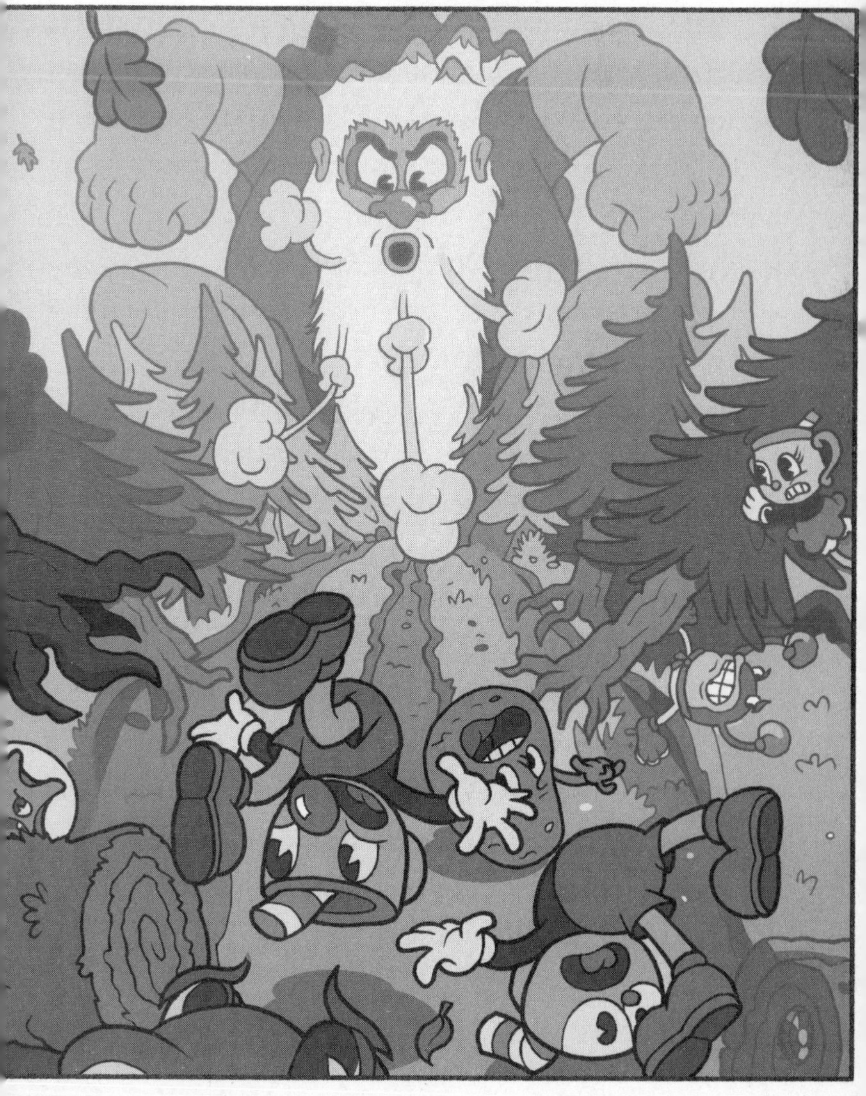

As for the rest of the campers, not only did they think it wasn't right—they were unquestionably certain it was wrong. And they weren't about to stand for it.

After all, the only reason the Punchafinks had lost was because they had abandoned the race to help rescue Mugman. It seemed no one was pleased with the situation, and it was causing quite an uproar. Then Ms. Chalice held up her arms.

"Gee whiz, nobody should lose their camp for doing a good deed," she told the group. "So I say we call it a tie!"

A tie! What a terrific suggestion! The contest would be finished, and there would be no winners and no losers. This was just the solution the campers were hoping for, and everyone howled and cheered and celebrated together.

At last, both camps were happy! It was a grand, wonderful, heartwarming ending, and also a very big mistake.

"A tie?" bellowed Glumstone, and the earth rumbled. "I never said anything about a tie! Look, I told you I'm sick of all the feuding and fighting around here! I said there could only be one camp, and one camp is all there's going to be! Now, which one is it?"

The campers suddenly grew quiet. This was a very serious question, and the mountain clearly meant to do what he'd promised. There seemed no choice but to sacrifice one of the camps. But which one? They pondered and pondered and—

"Destroy Hootenholler!" yelled Cora, sounding more like a pirate than ever. "It's only fair. They started it! We were minding our own business when they attacked our camp with buckets of gruel. This is all their fault!"

"That's not true!" said Cuphead. "All right, we may have dumped some gruel on your heads, and also hit the baroness in the face with a cake"—he always liked a good cake-in-the-face gag, and he wanted to make sure it wasn't forgotten—"but that's only after you wrecked our camp with one of your midnight raids! It was self-defense!"

Sal Spudder shook his head so hard he nearly peeled himself.

"Baloney! We didn't touch your camp until after you started it!"

"Did so!" said Ms. Chalice.

"Did not!" countered Ribby.

And then both camps got into a very loud argument, which completely obliterated the peace that had broken out only a short time earlier.

"Silence!" boomed the mountain.

The bickering stopped.

"See? This is what I mean," he said. "You are the noisiest bunch of campers a mountain ever had to put up with! Now, let's get to the bottom of this thing. Which camp hit the other one first?"

The Hootenhollers and Punchafinks all pointed at one another.

"It was them," said Cuphead. "That's the way Punchafinks are. They knew they had to mess up Hootenholler because we had the place lookin' too spiffy!"

"Spiffy, my eye!" groaned Cora. "Hootenholler's always been a dump, and it'll always be a dump!"

"That's only partially true!" said Mugman.

And then the arguing started all over again, only louder this time. All across the landscape, Hootenhollers and Punchafinks were angrily pointing their fingers and screaming at one another.

But just when things seemed at their worst, a voice—a very calm, quiet voice—interrupted the commotion.

"Excuse me. If I could have a word, please," said Tully, and the softness of his tone appeared to soothe the whole situation. "I hate to intrude, but I don't believe we've heard from everyone yet, and I think it's important that we do."

And then the little turtle turned and looked at a surprise witness—a witness who changed everything.

Slowly, the bus made her way to the center of the gathering.

"Do you have something you want to tell us?" Tully asked.

The old bus narrowed her headlights and lowered her grill and then sadly said, "I do—*chug, chug*—I do."

Now everyone stopped and listened.

"It was Quint—*chug, chug*. Quint did it—*chug, chug*.

Wrecked the camp—*chug, chug*. Said not to tell—*chug, chug*."

Every eye on the mountain turned and stared at Quint. The bus driver nervously looked at the campers, then put on his grumpiest scowl.

"All right," he muttered. "I did it. And I'd do it again!"

The crowd gasped.

"But why?" asked Cuphead.

"It was the curse!" Quint cried. "I had to do somethin'. The worst camp was gonna be destroyed. I mean, what's the point of bein' a camp bus driver if you got no camp to drive to? Anyway, I figured our only chance was to mess up Camp Punchafink so it would be worse than Hootenholler. So I faked a midnight raid to get things started, and, well, it sorta got outta hand."

Well, you could've heard a pine cone drop (but no one did, because even the trees were too stunned to make a sound), as it was as quiet on the mountain as it had been in many years. But then, quite unexpectedly, Baroness Von Bon Bon cleared her throat.

"On a, um, related note," she said, clearing her throat again, "I suppose if we're being totally honest,

I'm also partly to blame. You see, I'm the one who told my campers to retaliate, even after I knew Cuphead had been punished. I guess, deep down, I was afraid of the curse, too. Punchafink could never really be safe unless Hootenholler was in shambles."

For a moment, the campers just stood there staring blankly at one another, and you could hardly blame them. After all, a revelation this big took time to process, but once they realized what had actually taken place—

"You!" said Cuphead, pointing his finger at nearly everyone who was taller than him. "You did this! You ruined our summer!"

"Yeah!" Cora agreed. "The campers wouldn't even know about the curse if it weren't for the people in charge!"

"They're all to blame, but mostly Quint!" shouted Canteen Hughes.

Quint's face quickly fell into a frown.

"Hey! Maybe I started things, but I didn't tell ya to keep goin' back!" he said.

And before you knew it, campers were yelling at directors, and directors were yelling at counselors, and the air was filled with squabbling, quibbling, and ear-splitting unpleasantness.

"BE QUIET!" bellowed Glumstone, and then he puffed out his chest and blew.

Of course, being a mountain, he unleashed a mountain-size blow. The mighty wind tore through the group like a hurricane, and rocks and trees and bushes and gnomes were all caught in the terrible gale. The campers tumbled down the hill, as well, rolling and rolling until the great breeze finally halted.

"Gee golly!" said Cuphead. "When he blows his stack, he really blows!"

He was speaking to Ms. Chalice, but Ms. Chalice wasn't listening. She had turned her attention to an unusual sight lying at the foot of the mountain. You see, quite by accident, the two banners the groups had brought with them to signify their teams had become hopelessly twisted together.

Ms. Chalice and Cora looked at each other.

"Hootenfink!" they shouted.

"What are you talking about?" asked Cuphead.

Then he saw the banners. Sure enough, the two names had merged into one. The other campers noticed this, as well. And then and there, in a grand, united voice, the entire group gleefully cheered—

"CAMP HOOTENFINK!"

Wrongway turned to the baroness.

"You know, the real curse on our camps has been this silly feud. It's gone on too long and ruined too many summers."

"But if we join together, we can make a better camp for all of us!" the baroness said.

The two of them stared up at the mountain.

"You said you wanted just one camp. We can make that happen," Wrongway called out. "What do you say?"

The mountain rubbed his gigantic chin.

"Well, I don't know," he said, wrinkling his forehead. "I hate to see a good curse go to waste. It just doesn't seem to be in the spirit of the thing. And besides, even if you joined together with a new name and all, how do I know anything would really change? No, what I want is a place where campers live in—"

"Har-MO-neeeeeeee!"

The melodic word came out of nowhere, as if carried on the breeze.

"Exactly, that's just what I was going to say!" said the mountain. "Of course, not quite so musically."

Ah, but some words are made for music, as are some moments. And this being one of them, nobody was the least bit surprised when a certain very popular barbershop quartet popped out of a passing tumbleweed.

The Four Mel Arrangement had a special message for the gathering, and they delivered it in a tuneful croon (as was the style at the time).

WELLLLLLLLLLLLL—
When you TAKE TWO *camps and* ADD *a*
    CURSE—
(ADD *a curse*)
It ON-*ly* MAKES *things* GO *from* BAD *to*
    WORSE—
(BAD *to worse*)
The CAMP-*ers* FUSS *and* FEUD—
They're ROW-*dy and they're* RUDE—
But END *that* CURSE *and soon e-nough you'll* SEE—
(YOU *will* SEE)
They'll CHANGE *their* TUNE *and be in* HAR-MO-
    NEE!

HAR-MO-NY! HAR-MO-NY!
THAT'S *the* SOUND *of* VIC-TOR-Y!
BLEND TO-*gether and then* YOU'LL A-GREE—
SUMMER'S *better with some* HAR-MO-NY!

At this point, Mugman was so moved by the tune that he picked up two sticks and began playing a row of mushrooms like they were a set of drums. Unfortunately, he mistimed his last beat, so instead of striking a toadstool, he conked a gnome on the head. And while he felt awful about it, he did learn two important things about gnomes: They can be very forgiving, and if you hit them just right, they make a noise like a cymbal.

TA-CHIZZZZZZZZZZZZZZZZ!

NOWWWWWWW—
WHEN *the* HOOT-*en*-HOLLERS *had some*
    TROUBLE—
(GREAT *big* TROU-BLE)
The PUNCH-*a*-FINKS *came* RUN-*nin' on the*
    DOUBLE—
(ON *the* DOU-BLE)
They PUT *a-side their* RIFT—

And GAVE MUG-*man a* LIFT—
And PULLED *a* TRI-UMPH *out of* TRA-GE-DY—
*(*TRA-*ge*-DEE*)*
ALL *because they* FOUND *their* HAR-MO-NEE*!*
HAR-MO-NY*!* HAR-MO-NY*!*
THAT'S *the* SOUND *of* VIC-TOR-Y*!*
WANT *these* CAMP-*ers to live* PEACE-FUL-LY*?*
SING A-LONG *and* BRING *the* HAR-MO-NEE*!*

Well, you know what happens whenever the four Mels invite someone to sing along. Suddenly, the trees started swaying, and the rocks started rocking, and big, beautiful music notes magically burst out of the ground. A moment later, the clouds formed themselves into song lyrics, and the sun (who, being a star, could never resist a good show) bounced from word to word like a red rubber ball.

And then Cagney, Ollie, Quint, Wrongway, the baroness, the campers, the gnomes, and even the earthworms united their voices and joined the next chorus, which went something like this:

SOOOOOOOOO—
MIS-*ter* MOUN-TAIN, LIS-*ten, please—*

THERE'S *a* WAY *to make this* BOTH-ER *a*
  BREEZE—
AND *it's* SIM-*pler* THAN *you* THINK—
TURN *these two* CAMPS *into* HOOTEN-FINK*!*
HOO-TEN-FINK*!* HOO-TEN-FINK*!*
JOIN *to*-GETH-*er, it's a* NAT-U-*ral* LINK*!*
FIX *this* BROK-*en* SUM-*mer* IN *a* WINK—
HAIL *a* NEW TRA-DI-TION—HOO-TEN-
  FINNNNNNNNNK*!*
HOOTEN-FINK*!"*

When the song ended, and everyone had shouted
and cheered and clapped their hands, they all turned
around and looked hopefully at Glumstone.

"Oh, what the heck," he said at last. "Hootenfink
it is!"

22

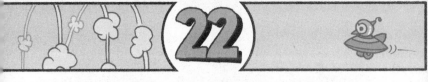

FOND FAREWELL

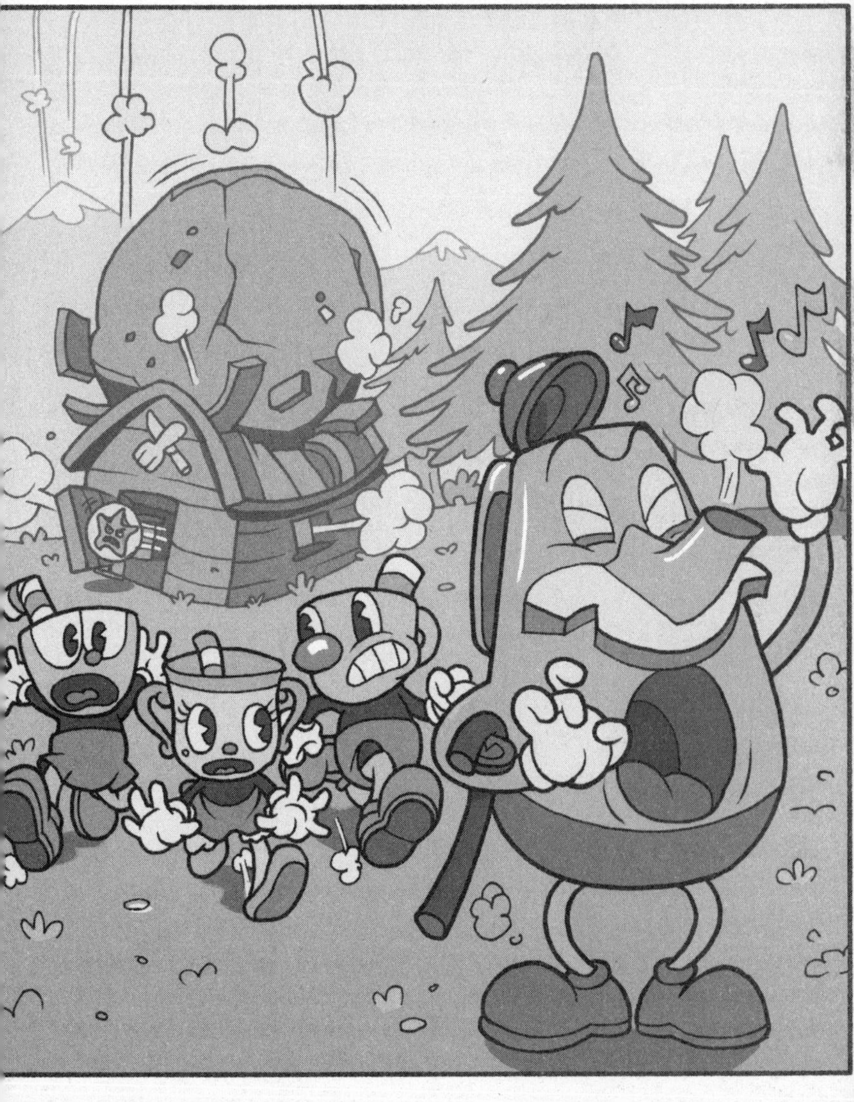

And so, for the rest of the summer, the campers did everything together, and the former rivals became the best of friends. What's more, they learned a great deal from one another—for example, Sal Spudder taught Cuphead how to build a raft, and Cuphead taught Sal how to make a hilarious disaster out of a bucket of gruel. And though he never did see any butler bears or treetop diving boards or bright neon signs, the camp turned out to be everything Cuphead had dreamed it would be, and maybe a little bit more.

The only thing the campers regretted was that it was over too soon. Fortunately, there was still one thing to look forward to: Old Camper's Day, the day when the campers from long ago came back and visited the place. Cuphead, Mugman, and Ms. Chalice were very excited to see Elder Kettle, and when he arrived, they told him all about their adventures and about the new name of the camp.

"Hootenfink?" Elder Kettle groaned, wrinkling up his nose. "Oh, I'm not sure how I feel about that. I mean, the *Hooten* part is all right. And I suppose it does have sort of a ring to it. HOOT-enfink. HOOTEN-fink. HOOTENFINK! You know, the more I say it, the more it grows on me. Yes, it's a fine name, a very fine name. And by George, it's just what this camp needed. I'm very proud of you, very proud of you all!"

And he was.

Meanwhile, Wrongway crossed the grounds (after someone turned him around and sent him in the right direction) and said hello to his old friend.

"Yo-Yo!" he said. "It's good to have you back at Camp Hootenholl—I mean, Camp Hootenfink!"

"Director Wrongway," Elder Kettle said excitedly, taking the compass by the hand. "Congratulations! The camp looks better than ever, and the campers have been telling me the wonderful news. Bringing the camps together is an excellent idea. And best of all, no more curse! Good riddance! That thing has been nothing but trouble for generations, and I, for one, am glad we no longer have to worry about boulders raining down from the sky. What a relief!"

And then they all chatted and laughed and reminisced about things that had happened long ago, because memories of camp never leave you—not even the ones that should. You see, caught up in the moment, Elder Kettle stepped onto a tree stump and relived the one memory he should have left back at the cottage.

"Elder Kettle! No!" the three friends yelled together, but it was too late.

"*YOO-dle, YOOOO-dle, YARG-EHHH-LARRRRRRRRR!*" he yodeled.

Needless to say, every camper turned and looked at him, and Elder Kettle was enjoying being in the spotlight again. That is, until a small shadow appeared overhead. And then it grew larger and larger and—

CRRR-ASHHHHHHHH!

The boulder fell out of the air and smashed the empty mess hall into a very messy pile of rubble.

"NO YODELING!" boomed a mountain-size voice from across the woods.

"Oh my," said Elder Kettle. "I must be more out of practice than I thought!"

And then they all laughed, and Wrongway promised a new and better mess hall would be awaiting them when they arrived next year. Then he stealthily looked around, just to make sure Ollie wasn't in earshot.

"Hopefully one with better food," he whispered.

And the campers laughed all over again.

Cuphead, Mugman, and Ms. Chalice spent the rest of the evening saying goodbye to their new friends and promising it wouldn't be long until they were all together again. And then young and old joined together around the campfire to sing songs and tell scary stories and roast the most delicious marshmallows any of them had ever tasted.

And when they'd sung every tune and told every tale and stuffed themselves to the point of bursting, Cuphead headed off to his bunk and went straight to sleep. Because even though this had been a very, very wonderful summer, it was never too early to start dreaming about the next one.

THE END? NOPE!

Now that you've survived all those camp shenanigans, go back for another look at the images and see if you can find these hidden objects, characters, and bosses. Good luck!

Hidden Objects

COIN X 22

POKER CHIP X 4

DICE X 4

Hidden Characters

LUDWIG X 1

MAC X 1

LUCIEN X 1

CHIP X 1

WOLFGANG X 1

SILVERWORTH X 1

Hidden Ghosts

GHOST X 1

GHOST X 1

GHOST X 1

GHOST X 1

GHOST X 1

Hidden Minions

CLOWN X 3

MOSQUITO X 3

MUDMAN X 3

MINI SLIME X 3

UFO DUCK X 3

STARFISH X 3

FIRE IMP X 1

CLOCKWORK MOUSE X 1

CANDY CORN X 1

PENGUIN X 1

WORKER BEE X 1

BONUS

Dastardly Difficult Expert Items

HORACE RADICHE X 1   CUPPET JR. X 1

ACKNOWLEDGMENTS

The more I thought about it, the more I realized there was something fitting about Cuphead's second novel being set at a summer camp. A camp, as you know, is a place where you gather with old friends and new friends for an incredible adventure that you'll remember all your life. This book was my camp.

Of course, the experience is only as good as the people you share it with, and in that department, I am one happy camper. This troop led me through the wilderness, steered me away from danger, dragged me up every hill, and kept me going when I thought I couldn't hike another step. But mostly, they entertained and enlightened me every single day, and in the process, they earned a very special place in my mental scrapbook.

It would take a work twice this size to tell you how thankful I am for the frighteningly fertile brains of Chad and Jared Moldenhauer. Somewhere in that amazing network of neurons, the Inkwell Isles were born, and the world became a much more magical place. The fact that I got to spend my days playing with Cuphead, Mugman, Ms. Chalice, and the other inhabitants of this fantastic land is a privilege I do not deserve. It's as if Chad, Jared, Tyler, Eli, and the ridiculously gifted group at Studio MDHR created a gigantic ice-cream sundae, loaded it with every imaginable topping, and then—for reasons entirely their own—let me put the cherry on top. I'm honored.

Naturally, I'm profoundly grateful to Rachel Poloski and the team at Little, Brown and Company for giving me the opportunity to go on this adventure. Rachel is the Swiss Army knife of editors, equipped with a multitude of talents and capable of deploying just the right skill at just the right time to solve any problem. This story was a collaborative journey from cover to cover, and one that wouldn't have been as satisfying or nearly as much fun without this remarkable crew. I'm not exaggerating when I tell you they made every idea stronger and every page better.

And then there's Brandi Bowles. I don't pretend to know the inner workings of an agent's world or how they do what they do. What I do know is that she makes my life easier, more productive, and better in myriad ways, and I'm very lucky to work with someone who is so astoundingly good at guiding this canoe through the literary waters.

Finally, I need to give an appreciative nod to Wile E. Coyote. Never has one villain's pain brought so much pleasure to so many. It is a tribute to Chuck Jones and Michael Maltese that this character has been the inspiration for a thousand plots, ploys, and pratfalls. Because of his exploits, I avoid cliffs, explosives, and any product that bears the name *ACME* (except on the page, of course, where they bring me ruthless joy).

So, to everyone who made this book possible, I had a great summer—and let's go camping again soon!

Sonia Browder

Ron Bates is a novelist who writes about secret laboratories, bullies, evil robots, toilet monsters, super plumbers, cafeteria tacos, and all the other things that make being a middle-school student so interesting. A former newspaper reporter and humor columnist, he is the author of *Cuphead in Carnival Chaos*, *How to Make Friends and Monsters*, *How to Survive Middle School and Monster Bots*, and *The Unflushables*. He also writes comic books, poems, and other stuff for kids who like to laugh. He lives in Texas.